Keturah, Mother of Virtue

Angelique Conger

Copyrights

Book Cover by Dar Albert
ISBN 978-1-946550-75-0[1]

1. https://www.myidentifiers.com/title_registration?isbn=978-1-946550-75-0&icon_type=Assigned

Table of Contents

New Life

The sun rose fiery red in the east that morning. I stood in the cold air shivering as I braided my hair, wondering at the meaning of the portent. Mother often told me the natural events of the heavens would lead to changes in my life. I did not often believe her.

I should have believed her that morning.

I dropped my braid to my back and turned as Mother approached. "Keturah, you are wanted at the big tent."

"The big tent? With Abraham and Sarah?" I shivered. "They are old people."

"Yes," Mother growled. "And our masters. We work for them. They provide our home, our food, and our work. Do not be disrespectful toward Sarah."

"I would never disrespect her or Abraham."

"See that you do not." Mother swatted me on my bottom. "They wait for you. But stop by the well and wash your hands and face before you get there. You do not want to present yourself to the Mistress with dirty hands and face."

I dutifully stopped and washed, in no hurry to present myself to the mistress.

Why do they want me? She is old. She always scowls at me. Why would she ask for me?

I pulled on my braid to straighten it and brushed at my clothing, swatting away any dust from my walk and ensuring it lay smoothly before I scratched at the tent door.

"There you are." Sarah's maid Dor beckoned to me. "We have been waiting for you. Come in."

I stepped through the door into a new life.

Two other young women moved about the room, cleaning and dusting Sarah's possessions. Sarah sat in a chair with a basket of wool at her feet, carding the lengths of it straight so it could be spun into fiber and woven into cloth. Although her hands were wrinkled with age, she kept them busy.

I ducked my head. "Mother said I am needed."

Sarah's voice was creaky and rough, as old women's voices are. "You are welcome, Keturah. I am in need of a new maid. Dor is to be married soon."

"And ... and ... you want me to be your maid?" I stuttered before lifting my head to glance into her ancient face.

Will I ever be as old and careworn as Sarah? Will I live well past one hundred years?

"I have watched you with your mother. Orpah is a good woman. She taught you well in the ways of caring for a home. Yet, am I right that she has not taught you to read or write?"

I stared at the toes of my shoes. "Mother did not learn to read or write. Her father saw no reason for a woman to have such skills."

"Women have many uses for *such skills.*" Sarah's voice hardened on the words mother often repeated from her father. "Your grandfather had no understanding of the needs of women. Few men do."

"Perhaps it is because he never learned to read himself," I whispered.

"Perhaps." Sarah's voice had become stronger, less creaky and rough as she used it. She softened it more. "Would you like to learn to read and write? I expect all my maids to have that skill. You seem intelligent, and I need an intelligent maid. I believe you will make a good one for me. Will you do that for me?"

I quickly reflected on my life, my dreams, my hopes, and the freedom I wished to gain when I had a home of my own. I loved walking in the hills among the sheep and goats. I doubted I would find time for that if I were tied to Sarah as her maid. But she offered opportunities I never hoped to have in my life.

My eyes wandered around the room, following the fingers of Avi as she dusted. She gently removed a book and dusted it, taking a moment to flip through the pages and read a word or two. I longed to be able to read. I had heard Sarah and Abraham had copies of sacred texts, including Adam's Book of Remembrance and the books written by the ancient matriarchs.

"Would I be able to read the stories written by the ancient matriarchs?" I popped my hand over my mouth. *How could I be so brazen?*

Dor stiffened, but Sarah laughed.

"You have heard of those books? Yes. I have copies. And, yes. You would be allowed to read them, after you learn to read, and after your other chores are completed. I believe it is important for women to know about the lives of our ancestors. These were your ancestors as well as mine." She reached a hand out toward me. "Does this mean you will accept?"

Thunder clapped, causing me to jump. It would rain soon.

I thought of Ezra in the fields with the other men. His kindness to me had saved me more than once. Would *the men rush from the fields out of the rain soon?*

"And if a man asks to marry me?"

"You are young still, are you not?" Dor asked.

I lifted my head. "Eleven, on my next naming day."

Sarah nodded. "You have a few days before it will be time to be concerned about men and marriage. However, I have always allowed my maids to marry and care for their own families when men come to call. I only ask that I be given the opportunity to ensure your young man is honorable."

I breathed out a tiny sigh. Ezra would pass her test, I was certain of it. Besides, she would teach me to read! "Then, yes. I will become your maid. When do you want me to begin?"

Rain pattered gently on the tent.

Sarah grinned, her face lighting up as if a ray of sunshine had somehow passed through the rain and the tightly closed tent door. "Would now be soon enough? You will be given a small payment."

Mother and Shet will take it from me.

"And I will give your parents a stipend for your time. Your mother and father depend on your labors. I must repay them."

That is why Mother was willing to send me here. She and Shet always look for payment.

"Shet is not my father. Mother married him when I was small." The rain pounded harder on the roof of the tent.

Sarah lifted an eyebrow. "Does he not care for you as a father?"

My eyes returned to my toes. "Sometimes. Sometimes he is unkind."

"Remember to love and respect him as a father. He will learn to be kind."

I doubt it. Shet has never been kind to me. "I will remember that."

Sarah's eyes seemed to stare through me as she considered me. "I have heard Shet has fits of anger and sometimes beats your mother. He is not one of us. He has not yet learned to treat a woman as Jehovah would expect."

I bit my lip. "He does not honor Jehovah, nor does he honor women."

"As I thought. Let me know if you have troubles because of him."

"You would —" I stopped. It would be disrespectful of me to ask if she would protect me from his sharp tongue and lashing whip.

"I would protect you, yes," she said.

"And now," Dor said, stepping closer, "you must begin to learn your duties. Yaffa will instruct you."

The portent of the red sky had not been wrong.

Serpent Skin

Life with Sarah and the other maids was easier than I expected it to be. Mother had taught me to cook and clean, so it was not a problem for me to do those tasks for Sarah. Yaffa and Avi were exceedingly kind in their willingness to show me what to do. Best yet, I would sit with the others in the afternoon while Sarah taught me to read and write.

Writing was a skill I kept to myself. I did not cherish the teasing I would receive from my brothers or Shet if they found out I was learning the skill. Sarah often told me I should be proud of it, but the teasing at home was cruel and unmerciful. I do not believe Sarah had ever heard the crudeness that emitted from Shet's mouth when others were not listening. I chose not to be his target and avoided it whenever possible.

At first, reading and writing made no sense to me. How could squiggly lines carry meaning? How could others interpret their meaning? It seemed to be magic to me. However, I knew Sarah and Abraham would not dabble in magic and Jehovah had commanded the prophets to keep a record of their actions and prophecies. Certainly, it was right and good.

I first read short sentences, then copied them onto a thin piece of bark with a sharpened stick burned at one end. The blackened point left marks on the bark that I soon recognized as letters and words. I graduated to scraps of vellum left from the books Abraham made.

Some of Sarah's books were written on a fine substance she called papyrus. She had used it in Egypt during the time she and Abraham lived there, waiting for the drought to end. One of Sarah's earlier maids,

Hagar, had made and sold the material from plants that grew along the edges of the Aur River, often running from the crocodiles. I always shivered when Sarah told us those stories.

We had predators there in the desert, but none like the crocodile with its sharp teeth and powerful jaws, hiding like a log in the water. Lions and hyenas stayed away from our camp, as did the serpents, most of the time.

Sadly, my work was seldom completed. Sarah would send me home after working through the long day, cooking and cleaning for her, expecting me to rest. Mother and Shet did not see it that way. As the only daughter, it was my responsibility to spend my evenings cleaning and cooking for them and my brothers. I had little time to slip away to talk with Ezra or wander into the hills.

One evening, Shet lay snoring in a drunken stupor on his bed and Mother sat in a daze nearby. The house was as clean as I could get it, until they woke, so I slipped out the door. I found Ezra standing near our tent, staring expectantly at the sky.

"I heard Shet's drunken snore. I hoped you would come out."

I set my hands on my hips. "Shet is not —"

"Not what? A drunk? Or snoring?" Ezra asked.

A loud snore echoed from within our small tent.

I grinned and lifted my shoulders in a small shrug. "A good man?" I whispered.

Ezra snorted. "I believe that. How can Abraham and Sarah allow him to continue to live here?"

I walked away from the tent a distance before I dared answer. Shet would beat me if he heard my answer. "He came as a servant from Abimelech. Then he married Mother. I suppose Abraham could not send him away when he helped to care for Mother and me. Now I have brothers."

"Care for you? All he does is drink any wine he finds and beat you and your brothers. I suspect he beats your mother as well."

"He brings us food, sometimes," I argued. *I do not know why I felt compelled to stand up for the wretched man.*

Ezra grabbed my elbow. "Come with me. I have something to show you."

"What is it?" Excitement filled me. I did not often see interesting things. That was for men and boys who left the village to herd the animals, work in the fields, or hunt animals.

"You will see." He led me out of the village a short distance to a quiet spot beneath a tree. On the ground lay a long, thin, black and white speckled skin of a serpent.

I yelped. "What is that doing there?"

"You are safe," Ezra laughed. "It is only the skin left by the serpent. He discarded it here when he outgrew it."

"They leave their skins behind?"

"They do. Touch it."

I warily stooped to touch the skin.

"Gently," Ezra warned.

I yanked back my hand. Ezra cackled. "It will not hurt you. It is only the serpent's skin. But it has lost the strength of the serpent. It can fall apart."

I brushed the skin lightly with one finger.

"You can touch it harder than that," Ezra said with a laugh. "Stroke it."

I shivered. I did not like serpents. But I enjoyed having Ezra near, so I let my fingers run along a distance of the skin. It felt dry and crackled beneath my fingers.

"I expected it to be slimy."

"No. That is something a silly girl would say. Serpents cannot be slimy in the dry desert sand. Be careful of serpents like this one. They climb trees and eat other serpents. They will rarely kill you, but their bite is painful."

"Why would they bite me?" I asked with wide-open eyes.

"These? Because they are cornered and cannot slip away. Others, because they are angry, horrible creatures."

I shivered. I did not want to see a serpent slithering through the grass or sand.

The next day, Sarah gave me a larger scrap of vellum. I used it to describe the serpent skin Ezra showed me. I wanted to remember our time together. I still have that scrap of vellum buried among my earliest writing.

Left Behind

Sarah kept me busy much of the day. For that, I was grateful. Although she worked me hard, my days with Sarah were pleasant, and I soon learned to read and write. However, my time in Mother's tent became a problem. My body matured, and I began to look more like a woman than a girl.

Shet noticed. His eyes darkened to black. My life became more miserable when he lunged toward me with grasping hands, seeking to touch me where he should not, trying to kiss me with his stinking, stale wine breath. I soon knew what he wanted and shrunk away from him, hiding whenever I could.

My younger brothers watched, then copied their father's lurid behavior, trying to trap me and kiss me. Some would even try to touch me with their man parts as he did. Our tent was small and crowded, leaving me nowhere to hide.

I found things to do to help Sarah later into the evening, then took my time returning to Mother's tent. *How could she allow Shet to treat me this way? How could she allow her sons, my brothers, to abuse me as they did?*

I knew. Mother took Shet as a husband when I was tiny because no one else would take her. Father had been an Egyptian servant who came with Abraham when he left Pharaoh's court. He must have been a good man to marry my mother, a heartless, unfeeling, and contemptible woman. When Father fell down a ravine and broke his leg, Mother did little to help him heal, nagging him to stand on the injured leg so he could get food for them.

The stench of green pus that soon filled the wound sickened Mother. Only then did she call for a healer. Too late, for Father did not live long. The healer, Refeala, told me Father's last days were painful and unhappy.

Shet moved in with Mother shortly after Father's burial in a local cave. Even as a little child, I could see Shet's cruelty. If Mother refused him something, his fist sent her flying across the tent. Even when she struggled to waddle across the floor, huge with my brothers, his fists held no mercy. It came as no surprise that she allowed him to take liberties with me. It kept his hands away from her.

I stayed away as late as I could, slipping in to find my bed after all the sounds of movement ended. That did not always help, for one of them would waken and grope in my direction.

At last, I refused to return. Abraham found me huddled outside their tent door, shivering in the cool air.

"Why are you here so soon, Keturah?" he asked, lifting me to my feet.

"I can no longer stay in the tent with Mother." I flinched away from his gaze.

"What is this? You are bruised."

I lowered my eyebrows. "It is nothing." Even I could barely hear my hesitant whisper.

"Nothing! Bruises are more than nothing." Abraham's voice was no whisper. He helped me into their tent. "Sarah, have you seen this before?"

"What?" she asked, rising from her bed and wrapping a robe around her body.

"Keturah has bruises on her arms and legs."

And on my body and within me.

"How did this happen?" Sarah asked.

I fell to my knees at her feet. "I have tried to be kind to Shet. I have worked to obey him and treat him as the father you believe him to be." Tears bubbled up and my voice filled with fear and grief. *Would she send me back to Mother and Shet?* "But Shet believes he can use me as a common ..."

I sniffed and stopped speaking. *What am I saying? Shet is the father of our home. I am required to honor and respect him.* I closed my mouth and stared at the rug between our feet. I was not worthy to stand on this fine rug.

"How long has this been going on?" Abraham demanded. "Did you know of it, Sarah?"

"I have not allowed Mistress Sarah to know," I cried. "Do not hit her because of my poor inability to hide from Shet's fist."

Abraham stared at me. "Just his fist. Keturah. Look at me."

I peeked up at him through dark hair fallen from its braid.

He gently took me by the chin and lifted my face. "Has he touched you in other ways?"

"Other ways, Master Abraham?"

"In ways he should only touch his wife?" Sarah asked in a voice harsher than I had ever heard before, although she tried to soften it.

Tears fell from my eyes. "I tried to stop him," I sobbed. "I did all I could to hide. Forgive me."

"Forgive *you?*" Sarah asked.

"Shet says I ask for it."

"Are you not but a child?" Abraham asked.

"I had my womanly ways last year," I mumbled.

"Still, you are a child." His voice grew low and dangerous. "How long has this been going on?"

I inhaled. "Since shortly after my womanly bleeding."

"That will not happen in my village," Abraham roared. "Sarah, take care of Keturah. I will attend to this." He stomped out the tent door.

I fell at Sarah's feet. "I am sorry. I did not intend to cause you problems. Forgive me," I wailed.

Sarah smoothed my hair back from my face. "It is not you. Abraham is angry with Shet. How could I have missed your pain?" She lifted my face with her finger and stared at the bruises.

"I am good at hiding the bruises. Mother has lotions that hide them. I have used them." I swallowed. "I left before I could find more this morning, or you would not know yet."

"It is good you did. You have suffered long enough."

I let my head fall as I wept, and Sarah ran her hands through my hair until I calmed.

"You should wash your face and brush your hair. You will feel better," Sarah said.

I rose and washed my face.

"I have no brush. I left it at Mother's," I said.

"Use mine."

"Yours?" My head twisted toward her.

"You are welcome to use it for now. Brush and braid your hair before the other girls arrive. You do not want them to ask questions. This is a problem for you, not them. You do not need their gossip."

I nodded and lifted her brush to my hair. Enough women whispered gossip about Mother and Shet as I passed them in the village.

Shouting rose from outside the tent. My mother.

"Keturah! Keturah! Get out here. If we must leave, you must go with us," she screamed.

I tied my braid at the end and stumbled toward the tent door.

"You need not leave," Sarah said. "You are my maid. I would not have you leave."

"Where will I live if not with Mother?"

"We will solve that later. You do not have to face her."

"No. I must see her, see what my actions have caused."

"It is not your actions," Sarah said.

"Still, I must see." I lifted my head and walked outside.

"There you are," Mother yelled, scorn filling her voice. "I do not know what you told the master, but you have said enough. He has thrown us out." She surged forward to grab my arm. "Come with me." She yanked on my arm.

"No, Mother. I am not leaving Sarah. I am her maid. You gave me to her."

"To work for her, not to be her daughter! Now we are expelled from this land. Come. You must pack."

"I have little of value in your tent."

"Not your things, you stupid girl. You must prepare my things to leave."

Abraham strode between us and lifted her hand from my arm. "She is required to do no such thing. You have no further claim on this girl."

"She is my daughter," Mother screeched.

"You lost that privilege when you allowed your husband to use her so. You were told to pack and leave. You have one hour to be gone. You are wasting time."

"Keturah." Mother growled. "If you do not come with me now, I will take all your possessions with me."

I did not want to leave with her, but what would I do? Panic filled me.

"Do not fear," Abraham said. "Sarah and I will provide."

"Choose now," Mother yelped. "Me, your mother, or ... or ..." she stabbed her finger toward Sarah's tent. I glanced toward the tent. Sarah stood at the door.

"Her." Mother's voice dripped with contempt.

I do not know to this day how Mother made the word 'her' sound so ugly. Sarah straightened her ancient back and gazed calmly at Mother. "You are welcome with us, Keturah," Sarah said.

My head turned back and forth. Sarah. Mother. Who would I choose?

"Now!" Mother yelled. "I have no time for this. Come with me." She gripped my arm once more.

"No, Mother," I cried. "You refuse to protect me. I cannot go with you." I jerked my arm from her grasp and stepped back. "I choose to stay as Sarah's maid. Abraham will protect me."

A dark ugliness crossed my mother's face. "You would leave me for *them*? You are no longer my daughter. Stay here. See what happens to you. No man will have you. You will become an outcast, wandering alone in the desert."

I shrunk back. *Would I?* I shook my head. "No. Sarah and Abraham are honorable. I will stay here."

"Do not come crying to me, then," Mother spat, then turned on her heel and marched away.

I stared after her, trembling, until Sarah stepped to my side and put an arm around me. Abraham moved to my other side.

"You are safe here with us," Sarah said.

"We will not allow them to hurt you again," Abraham said with a scowl.

We watched as Mother and Shet gathered their things. Soon they and their sons scurried out of the village, dripping possessions behind them. Shet's dog snarled at any who followed.

New Home

I crept through my chores that day, fearful that Sarah and Abraham would change their minds and I would be left alone, with no one to protect me. Where would I sleep? What would I do? How would I be treated by the others?

Tears leaked from my eyes as I dusted and cleaned. *What would I do for clothing, a brush, a bed? Where would I sleep at night? Would my mother miss me?* Would I miss her? I wiped the tears from my eyes with the back of my hand. *All because I ... No. I cannot continue. I will find a way. Sarah said ... No. I cannot depend on her. I am not her responsibility.*

I stepped out of the tent in the middle of the morning and walked in the direction Mother's tent had been located, hoping to find a dress, a brush, a shoe? Anything of mine. The space was cleared. Nothing remained. I had nothing left.

I sucked in a shuddering breath and returned to Sarah's tent. It was time to help prepare the midday meal.

"I have a dress you can have," Avi murmured to me. "You are smaller than me, and it was my favorite. I grew out of it."

"A dress?" I asked.

"You remember. My blue dress."

I loved that dress. "You would give it to me?"

"Yes. You will need clothes to wear. I cannot wear it now." She lifted a shoulder in a shrug. "You are welcome to it."

"Thank you." I rolled my lips inward, fighting back sudden tears. "I would love to accept the dress."

"It will look good on you, with your gray eyes. I will get it for you during Sarah's resting time."

Sarah had become less healthy in the last few weeks and started resting in the afternoon during the time we had used for reading and writing. Until that day, I continued to practice writing or read from one of the books on Sarah's shelves. I had read through most of Eve's book the day before. I hoped to finish it soon. Now, my stomach churned. Would I ever be allowed to read the last of it?

Too many questions. Too many tears.

I wiped away my tears once more and bent to help with the meal.

Yaffa tucked a brush into my pocket. "Your dark hair is lovely," she whispered. "You will need a brush."

I gulped back the tears once more. "Thank you."

We carried food in for Sarah and Abraham. As I set a plate in front of Abraham, he asked me to wait. I stood quietly while they prayed.

Abraham addressed me. "A tent will be set up near here for you to use," he said. "Danil is locating one and will have it ready for you soon. It will not be large, only big enough for one person."

"A tent for me?" I asked.

"You will need a place to sleep," Sarah said. "I believe Bara is preparing a bed for you as well."

I bit the inside of my mouth to fight back the tears springing to my eyes. "Thank you. How can I repay you?"

"You can continue to help me care for my sweetheart wife," Abraham said. "You have been kind to her and treated her well."

I gawked at him. "I will be pleased to do that. I am grateful to be here with you." I turned to her. "I love you, Sarah."

"I can tell," Abraham said. He patted my hand. "Now, go eat. We will talk later."

As I sat to eat, men toted a tent past us. They set it up near Sarah's weaving tent. Bara and some other women followed soon after the tent was ready. They brought a bed, blankets, and a pillow. One woman brought a basket and left it inside the tent. A man brought a small table, his small son carried a stool. Others streamed past with baskets or bags, quietly depositing them inside the small tent.

I sat in amazement. *I am nothing. Less than nothing if I am to believe Shet. Mother and Shet have been the object of gossip all my life, and all these people are bringing me gifts? What did I do to deserve this?*

Avi left our table and hurried away, returning soon with her blue dress. She quietly slipped inside the tent and left it there.

We returned to help Sarah, and I tried to think of her needs rather than my own. We carded and spun wool together, preparing the thread to weave the following day.

"Do you like your new tent?" Sarah asked.

"I have not entered it yet," I said. "I did not know if I was allowed."

She tipped her head back and giggled. "It is your tent, brought here for you. Go now. Look at it. Avi, go with her."

I set my spindle in the basket and strode out the door. Avi followed me.

"Are you nervous?" she asked.

I nodded, not trusting my voice to answer.

At my tent, I pushed the door back and peeped in.

"Go inside," Avi encouraged.

I stepped in. Someone had spread the bed out along one edge spread with colorful blankets. The table and stool sat beside the wall along the other side. I pulled the brush Yaffa had given me from my pocket and set it on the table beside a small circle of polished copper.

One basket held clothing. Another held a towel and a bit of soap. Avi's blue dress lay atop a small trunk.

I picked up the dress and held it in front of me. "This is so pretty."

"Wear it tomorrow," Avi said.

I knuckled my eyes once more. "How can I thank everyone for this?"

"Be the kind girl you have always been," Avi said. "We have seen your struggles. I suspected Shet was hurting you, but you hid it so well. I did not want to cause you greater problems." She put her arms around me and hugged.

"You saw? And you still like me?"

"Shet is horrible. We could see he treated you badly. I wondered how long you would accept it. I could not have accepted it for so long."

"I finally broke last night."

"It is time you did."

Late that evening, I crept into my new tent after eating with Avi and Yaffa, as usual. Even with all the gifts provided to me by my neighbors and friends, the tent felt spacious. I twirled in the center. *How do I deserve so much space? I even have a bed.* Mother and Shet had not provided me with a bed in her tent. I had a blanket which I wrapped around me and found a corner away from the others to curl in at night. Now, I had a bed with warm blankets, and a trunk and baskets filled with clothing and other possessions! I considered myself wealthy.

I touched everything in the baskets and trunk, amazed at the kindness of the men and women of Mamre. They had never treated me well before. Perhaps they were held back by Mother and Shet. Their misery and unkindness kept people far away.

I thought they hated me, for I heard my name connected with theirs often in their gossip. I seldom heard more than a whisper, with Mother's or my name floating into recognition. But I could tell they spoke of me as they peeped above hands that covered their mouths.

How could they treat me so kindly after gossiping about me before? It made no sense.

I sprawled on the bed, amazed at the opportunity to stretch out my arms and legs. It had been years since I could extend my arms and legs without touching another person.

And the quiet. No one spoke, no one shouted, no one argued or complained. Just me, and I had nothing to disagree about, no one to differ with. I thought I had gone to heaven.

Did others live this way? Certainly they must, for I had worked for Sarah for many months now and I never heard them raise their voices, not even toward servants or other workers.

As darkness engulfed my tent, I lit a candle and knelt to pray. I thanked Jehovah for the kindness of others and the opportunity to continue to live in Mamre under Abraham's protection.

I blew out the candle and slipped into the bed, relishing the softness of the clean blankets, and soon slept.

Yet, something woke me.

A noise outside my tent. *Is someone trying to get in? Who is it? What do they want?*

I stretched my hearing as far as I could. A scratch sounded against the outside of the tent. My heart thumped loudly in my ears. All I could hear was my heart.

Is it Mother or Shet returning to hurt me? A man coming to take advantage of me alone in my tent? What is out there?

I pulled my robe close around my sleeping dress and stepped close to the tent door, breathing deeply to calm my heart and listening. I heard the scratching sound again. I sucked in another deep breath. My hand quivered as I reached for the door to pull it back.

Inhaling once more, I opened the door and stood staring out.

"Keturah," Ezra whispered. "Why are you awake?"

"I heard a sound. It woke me. I feared Mother or Shet had returned."

"It was me. I am part of the guard who walks through the village each night. We ensure no one causes problems for others here during the night. I bumped into something."

"Are you here every night?"

Ezra's teeth gleamed in the moonlight as he grinned. "Not me every night, but someone is. Three of us patrol every night. We take turns. You are safe here."

"I did not know that. Shet never did."

He shook his head. "No. Shet would not be invited to participate in guard duty. We could not trust him."

"He would allow our enemies into our village?"

"I have no way of knowing that," Ezra said, shuffling his feet. "I have only been part of the guard patrol for a few months. I am not part of the leadership. But I never saw Shet participate, even when I went out with Father."

"He was always drunk," I said with a growl. "Even if he had been assigned, Shet would have missed attending. And he would never have noticed any danger."

"I heard that," Ezra murmured. He held his hands up to protect himself in case I became angry. "He is your father. I am sorry."

"I am sorry he was considered my father. He was not. He did nothing to deserve that title. I am glad he is gone."

"You will not miss your mother?" he brushed the hair from his eyes. "I would miss my mother if she left me behind."

I allowed the air to rush from within me. "I do not know if I will miss her. Perhaps, but I do not believe I will. Too much grief happened in her tent. She never even tried to protect me." I bit my lip. "I said too much. I may miss Mother, eventually."

"Sad," Ezra said. "I must go or the others will come looking for me. You are safe."

I watched as he bravely marched away, gazing into the dark corners. With him and the others out there in the night, I did not have to fear Shet's return in the middle of the night.

I returned to my bed and slept soundly.

Dreams

Over the next months, Sarah's health declined. She spent more time in her bed resting and less time in her weaving tent. Avi and Yaffa joined me in her care, often speaking of our concern for her health. When Abraham and Isaac left to sell the wool, we took turns sleeping on the floor near her bed so we could help her.

One night when it was my turn to sleep next to Sarah, she was restless and cried out in her sleep.

I touched her hand. "Sarah," I whispered. "Sarah, are you well?"

She shuddered and gripped my hand. "I do not know. My heart is racing. I must have been sleeping."

I nodded. "Yes, you were sleeping."

She swallowed. "And I was dreaming."

"Dreams can be frightening," I said, trying to soothe her.

"This one was." She shuddered.

I watched her face as fear and horror filled it. Then she shook her braids. "But as I think of it, the dream is not as bad as it seems." She pushed up onto her elbow. "It was strange."

"Would you like to tell me about it?" I asked, uncertain I wanted to hear.

She leaned back. "Maybe not. You are young. You do not need to hear such horrible things."

"Horrible things? In your dreams? Are they real?"

"Real enough. I remember too many bad things in my life. They must have mixed together." Her laugh seemed forced. "You do not know about bad things. I should not hurt you."

I laughed. "I do not know about bad things? Do you not remember why I am here in Mamre alone?"

Sarah grinned at me. "Yes. You have encountered pain. My torments are different from yours."

"I suspect that in a few years, I will think less of my grief. Shet has been gone for a time. When more time has passed, perhaps I will no longer consider them every day."

"Your experiences were terrible."

"And your dream must have been awful, for you cried out in your sleep." I patted her hand. "Are you certain you do not want to share?"

She cleared her throat and stared at the ceiling.

"I dreamed Abraham took Isaac with him to a mountain to sacrifice."

"That is nothing new. Has he had Isaac help him with the sacrifices before?"

Sarah stared at the top of the tent for a long while before speaking. "He has. But this was different. Pharaoh stood at the base of the mountain laughing. Then Abimelech joined him, pointing and mocking. That is bad enough. But they took no sacrificial lamb, only the wood to burn the sacrifice."

My breath caught in my throat. "No lamb? What would they sacrifice?"

"Exactly my question. What did they plan to sacrifice? Isaac went willingly, helping his father to climb the mountain, carrying the wood on his own back, pointing at the birds and clouds in joy. But ..." Her voice trailed off.

"It was only a dream, Sarah! Abraham would not take your only son ..." I could not say the words. The pain stopped my voice as it had quieted Sarah.

"No. He could not. His father tried to sacrifice him to Elkenah many years ago. Neither of us could understand how a father would do that, especially to a false god. But Jehovah is not the false god. He is the true and living God. He would not ask that of Abraham, of me!" Sarah's eyes were wide and her voice wild. "Would he?"

"How could he ask for your only son?" I spoke softly, seeking to calm her beating heart bouncing her wrist against my hand and in her throat in the dim light. "He is a loving God. Jehovah would not do that."

Sarah inhaled deeply and slowly let it out, then did it again. "He promised me a son. He promised us as many children as sands on the seashore. I suppose He could give us another child. But I am past one hundred years old. I do not want to think of carrying another child at my age. It was difficult enough before when I was ninety."

I giggled. "Back when you were young."

Sarah giggled with me. "That sounds funny, although it is true."

"I was not yet born when you carried Isaac. I am but thirteen years."

"And Isaac is twenty-three, ten years older than you."

"Isaac is a good man. I have watched him with his father. He is gentle and kind."

"He is." Sarah leaned back on her pillow.

I hoped she would soon forget the bad dream.

"I do not understand," she murmured. "Why would Pharoah and Abimelech stand and mock?"

"Perhaps because they think their idol gods have prevailed over Jehovah. If they can convince Abraham to sacrifice Isaac?"

"Perhaps. However, they do not know the mind and will of Jehovah. They have not yet learned that all is possible for Jehovah." Her voice slurred with sleepiness. "If Jehovah were to take Isaac, He could bring him back to life. He is mightier than any idol ..." Her voice slipped from a whisper into nothingness. She slept once more.

I sat holding her hand and thinking for a long time. She had such great faith. I would have been screaming at Jehovah not to take my child, especially since it took so long to get Isaac. But no. Sarah considered all the ways Jehovah could resolve the problem if he took her only son after promising a multitude of posterity.

I resolved to be more like Sarah.

I lay back on my blanket and pulled it over me, thinking of Sarah's actions in the years since I came to be her maid. She was unfailingly kind. Even when I did something without thinking, she offered kindness in her correction. I only heard the roughness of anger when Abraham sent Mother and Shet away. And that was short-lived, followed by concern for me and my welfare.

How did she do it? How could she be so kind when people failed her?

Sarah had years to practice, many years. I could be like her. I could become as filled with godliness as she was.

I determined to watch her, to listen to her more closely. I wanted to be like her.

Shet appeared in the doorway of my little tent. "You thought you could get away from me? Abraham cannot always be here to protect you."

My eyes opened at the harshness of his voice. *How did he get past the patrol?*

"Shet?" my voice rasped from sleep and fear.

"Keturah. I have missed you."

"How did you —?"

"Get past the guard? You forget. I lived in this village for many years. I know how to hide from the guards. How do you think I got all the wine? That slime, Abraham, refused to provide us with the all wine we needed."

I had heard this complaint from Shet. He did not understand Abraham's need to have his herders sober when they were responsible for the animals.

"Do not stand up for the man," Shet growled. "I know you love him more than me."

Love him more than you? Any love for another man, even an enemy, would be more than for you. I despise you. I knew better than to say anything. Instead, I scooted back until I felt the tent against my back.

"You cannot get away from me," Shet said. He advanced toward me, reaching out to grab me.

I tried to scream, but could make no sound.

Shet just laughed. "You cannot get away from me."

My heart raced. *How could I get away from him? What could I use to protect myself? Sarah and Abraham had both told me I did the right thing when I ran from Shet. Would they agree I could hit him with something? What could I use?*

My hands scrabbled into a basket, searching for something I could hit him with. I did not own a club or a staff with which to bludgeon him. Nothing hard in that basket. I searched with my hands for something, anything. As my hand cautiously reached out, I could feel the cool, smooth surface of the night jar beneath my fingertips. The darkness enveloped me, and the only sound that broke the stillness was the faint rustle of footsteps. The night jar held urine from the night. *Nasty. But it will work.*

I tried to shout again, but, once more, my voice would not work.

"You cannot shout. You will get no help. The guard is far from here. He will not return for some time." Shet sneered at me. "And you know both Abraham and Isaac are gone. I saw them leave two days ago."

"They could return early," I whispered.

"They could, but they will not."

Time stretched out. Shet was in no hurry. He had all the time he wanted. He reached toward me, gripping my night dress.

"Take this off," he ordered.

"N... no." Sarah said I did not have to respect and obey him. "I will not."

Shet's fist raised. "I said, take it off," he growled. "I am not afraid to hit you."

It would not be the first time.

"No." I said it aloud, loud enough for him and anyone outside my tent to hear.

"You can shout. No one will hear you." Shet stepped closer and reached for my night dress. "I told you to take this off."

I lifted the night jar and stood with my back against the tent. "No. You cannot force me to do this anymore."

"No?" Shet sneered.

How can I see his face so clearly in the darkness of my tent?

His fingers caught my dress. I tugged on it, trying not to spill the night jar. "Let go! Leave me alone!" I tried to scream, but the sound would not come as loud.

I swung the jar toward his head. He yelped.

"What did you do that for, Keturah?" The voice was not Shet's.

"You are trying to hurt me," I cried. My voice worked once more.

"I would not hurt you, Keturah. I heard you cry out and came to see what the problem was. You were moaning and crying out in your sleep."

"Shet? What did you say?"

"I am Ezra, not Shet. He is long gone from our village."

I blinked my eyes several times. I crouched next to the tent wall with the empty night jar in my hands. What had happened? "Ezra? You are not Shet?"

"Do I sound like Shet?"

"No." I blinked again and rubbed my eyes with the back of one hand. Ezra had left the tent flap open, letting moonlight enter my tent.

"Set the pot down. I would feel safer if you did not hold it so. You look like you are ready to hit me with it."

"I was ready to hit Shet with it. He was here in my tent. He said he knew how to slip past the guards and no one would stop him."

"Shet was not here. You must have been dreaming." Ezra reached out and took the jar from me. "Is that why you threw the contents of your night jar at me?"

"Did I?"

"Smell me."

I leaned forward and sniffed. He stank. "I am sorry. It was all I had to protect myself against Shet."

"You must have had a terrible dream."

I lowered myself to a squat. "It was." I shuddered at the memory. "It seemed so real. He woke me and ..."

"He will not get to you. We watch closer here than anywhere else, because this is where Abraham and Sarah live. Shet will not sneak past. I will tell my leaders of your fear. We will watch your tent more closely."

"You will?" I struggled still to understand.

"Of course. You are important to Abraham and Sarah. We will protect you." Ezra moved back toward the door.

"I am only Sarah's maid."

"But you *are* her maid. That makes you important to them. We will come by more often. I must go home and change. My mother will not be happy about my stinking clothing."

I dropped my head. "I am sorry. I did not know it was you."

"I know. Dreams can seem real." He stepped out the door. "Try to get some rest. The sun will rise soon." He dropped the tent flap.

I sat on my bed and stared into the dark, thinking about the dream, if it was a dream. I needed a way to protect myself if Shet ever did come back. I would not be depending on a night jar for safety next time.

Avi and Yaffa laughed when they heard about my dumping the night jar on Ezra during the night. Sarah did not laugh when she heard the dream that brought him to my tent.

"Dreams can sometimes be warnings of things to come," she said.

"Was yours?"

Her face lost all color. "I do not know. I fervently hope not."

"As I pray my dream was not a warning. What should I do?"

Sarah stared at me. "What do you think you should do?"

I giggled. "Keep a full night jar near my bed."

At Sarah's stern gaze, I stopped giggling. "I need to have something within reach at all times, not just in my bed. Shet is vicious and cruel. He will return and try to hurt me. He will blame me for his and Mother's expulsion from Mamre."

"Your belt knife?" Sarah asked. "We all carry a knife on our belt."

I nodded. "Yes. And mine will reside under my pillow where I can find it at night. I will not be found helpless, searching for something for protection again."

I made a habit each night after that of tucking my belt knife under my pillow after my prayers.

Attack

Weeks later, the memory of the dream dimmed, but I did not forget. I moved the bed to face the door. I would not be surprised by a visitor. Each night I slipped my knife beneath my pillow, and I often slept with my hand holding it. It was good I did, for my eyes opened wide one night when I heard my tent flap scraping back late one night.

Light from outside illuminated the intruder — Shet. My dream flashed back. I knew what to do. I would not depend on the night jar, but it was available if I needed it. I fought to keep my breathing slow.

"There you are, Keturah," Shet whispered, his voice slurring with the wine I smelled on his breath. I hated that smell.

I gripped my knife, waiting to see what he would do. My heart beat increased. What would he do to me?

"Your mother wants to see you. Come with me. I will take you to her," he said, stepping closer to me.

"No. I do not want to see her. She left me." I sat up on the edge of my bed, pulling my blanket across my lap. I gripped the knife beneath the blanket. I continued to slow my breathing.

Shet pushed a stool into the tent doorway, to allow in the moonlight. "Orpah misses you. Come with me."

"Why are you coming here at night?" I asked. Mother would not care to see me. Not after my actions drove her and Shet out of the village.

"Abraham's guards will not allow me into the village during the day, even when I promised I would not hurt you." He snorted. "I suppose they had reason."

"How did you get past them?"

Shet's grin frightened me. "That boy, Ezra, is no match for me. He lies behind a tent."

I inhaled sharply. "Ezra. Did you kill him?"

"No, just hit him on the back of the head. He will live." He leaned close to me. "You like this Ezra."

"He is my friend." I moved the knife to my side, where I could easily use it. It would do me no good if it were tangled in my blanket.

"He will never hold you like I do. He is a boy. I am a man. He will wonder where you went. Come. You are going with me."

"A man who uses little girls," I cried. "Where is Mother? I thought you said she is nearby." I did not want him near me. I set my feet on the ground so I could move easily.

"She is. She is outside the camp. She cannot sneak in like I can."

I shook my head. "I do not want to see her again. She left me."

"Because that lout, Abraham, sent us away." Shet forgot to be silent in his frustration. "He would not have sent us away if you had not come a-crying to him. I have every right to do what I desire with or to you. You are the daughter of my wife." By the time he said all this, he was nearly shouting.

Perhaps Abraham will hear, or one of the guards.

"You had no right to do those things to me," I said, no longer trying to be quiet. "You are not my father. I am not your wife."

He raised his hand to slap me. I pulled my knife from beside me. "You will not slap me ever again."

His face hardened. "You think you can hurt me with your little knife?" His hand snaked forward to grab the knife from me, but I thrust my hand toward him. He missed me. I did not miss him. I hit him in the stomach.

"You stabbed me," Shet yelped.

I pulled the knife back, ready to strike him again. "And I will again if you do not leave."

He grabbed his stomach. Blood dripped from between his fingers. "You bitch. You hurt me. You think Abraham will want a girl who stabs her father? He will send you away. We will not take you back."

"Go! I would not want to return to your family if you were the only ones left in the desert," I shouted. "Leave me."

Shet lunged toward me, one hand holding his stomach, the other out to grab me. He caught hold of my nightdress as I leapt away. The night dress tore, leaving me standing near the tent wall nearly naked. Shet shook my dress.

"You have matured since we left. I will take you now, before I drag you away with me."

"You will not." I ground my teeth. "Not without being cut again. Try to hold two parts of your body together and take me with you still. I will slice you again and again."

I will cut his arm, I will cut his legs, I will cut anything I can reach.

Shet tucked my night dress into his stomach injury, then darted toward me. I stepped aside. He tripped on the trunk and cursed. Regaining his balance, he lunged forward again. I danced out of his reach, moving toward the tent door, putting the table between us.

"You cannot get away. No one will help you."

"I no longer care," I growled. "If I must slice you over and over, I will. You will never hurt me again."

Shet's laugh did not sound so certain. "You are just a girl."

"A girl with a knife. A girl who will never be beaten or abused by you again." I held my knife up and ready as I moved closer to the door.

"A girl who will not need to use that knife again on you," Isaac said as he pushed through the tent door. "What are you doing here, Shet? You do not belong here, or even in our village. I distinctly remember Father sending you away."

"I came back to see my daughter," Shet whined.

"I am not your daughter," I declared as I grabbed a blanket from the basket at my feet and wrapped it around me.

"You are not her father," Isaac agreed. "You lost that privilege when you abused her. She is free of you and the woman who bore her." Isaac stepped forward and grabbed Shet by the arm. "You will go with me."

Two other men stepped in, crowding my tent. I backed up against the wall. One of the men grabbed Shet's other arm while the other stepped behind him. Shet cried out in pain as they wrenched his hands behind him. My bloody night dress fell to the floor.

"I will bleed to death if you do that," Shet yowled. "She stuck me!"

"You deserve it," Isaac grunted.

The men tied his hands while Isaac picked up the dress and shoved it next to his stomach. "No need for you to bleed more onto Keturah's floor." He glanced at me. "Keturah, do you have something I can use to hold this on?"

I found a towel and handed it to Isaac with an outstretched hand, staying as far from Shet as I could.

Isaac wrapped the towel tightly around Shet's stomach and tucked it in so it would not fall off, then nodded to the other men. I stood back as they marched Shet from my home.

I turned around and stared at what had been my safe space, then grabbed a dress from a hook and pulled it over my head and tucked the knife into the belt before rushing outside. How could I return?

I sat on a rock near the path and sighed. Now what?

Sarah stepped out of her home and came to sit next to me. "Did you have your knife close?"

I nodded.

"And you stabbed him with it?"

I nodded again. A tear formed in the corner of my eye and rolled down my cheek.

"Good for you. You were prepared for this. No night jar spilled?"

I shook my head and giggled softly. "No night jars were spilled. But I stabbed him in the stomach."

"Maybe he will learn to stay away from places he is not wanted."

I grinned. "I hope so. He is never wanted, and never welcome, near me."

"I hope he learned that today."

"Me, too."

We stared eastward as the sky lightened above the hill with a golden glow. The day would be beautiful. I wish I could feel beautiful inside. How long would it take to overcome this attack?

"We marched Shet out of the village," Isaac told me later as I served his morning meal along with Abraham and Sarah.

"Did you have someone care for his wound?" Sarah asked.

"Yes. We took him to Refaela. He whined and cried all the while she cleaned the injury and stitched it back together. You did a good job stabbing him. Refaela says he may live. He limped off to his horse when we let him go at the edge of the village."

"Was my mother there?" I had to know.

"No. I did not see her. She may have been somewhere nearby, but we did not see her."

I growled deep in my throat. "He lied to me again. It does not surprise me. He thought he could get me to go with him to see my mother. I do not trust him."

"He is rather undependable," Sarah said.

"Rather." I barked a short laugh. "My mother is as bad. They deserve each other. I hope she lives to enjoy him."

"I hope she lives as well," Abraham said. "She would not deserve a death at his hands, even if she has treated you poorly."

I shook my head and picked up the empty serving bowl. "Mother deserves Shet, I am sorry to say. I, however, do not."

"It is good you were prepared," Isaac said. "What made you think to have your belt knife beneath your pillow?"

"A dream. I dreamed this happened one night, but I did not have my belt knife and was forced to hit him with my night jar. I decided the next morning to always have my knife close."

"Argh," Abraham said with a shiver. "That would not be pleasant."

"It was not for Ezra. He walked in on my dream and the contents of my night jar splashed over him."

"I remember that night," Isaac said with a laugh. "Ezra shivered and stunk the rest of the night. We told him he should not interrupt a woman's nightmares."

"It felt worse than a nightmare," I said, ducking my head and slipping out of their tent.

Shet's attack had been worse for him than it was for me. I lost a night dress, but it was not one I cared for, much. Better to lose a night dress than to be attacked and dragged away from home. Thank Jehovah, I was safe.

We did not see Shet or my mother again. I often prayed for her safety. Only Jehovah and Mother know.

Sacrifice

A year passed. Sarah's health did not improve. She sometimes rose from her bed to work in her weaving tent, but not as often as she had before. She did not have the strength for it. Still, she insisted on weaving for a time almost every week.

Abraham's health was not much better than hers. His stooped walk forced me to recognize it. Still, he occasionally went to the hills with the sheep, and regularly took part in discussions about selling the wool. Isaac often took his father's place on sales journeys. Abraham would sit under the cedar tree and stare into the clouds.

Then early one morning, as the sky streaked with red clouds, Abraham took Isaac and a few servants and left the confines of our village.

"Where are they going?" I asked Sarah, who stood in the door to their tent watching them leave.

"They go to sacrifice."

"Could they not sacrifice here as they have done before?"

"They could, but Jehovah commanded Abraham to go to Mount Moriah."

I stood watching them leave. Only Abraham rode, and he rode a donkey instead of his white stallion.

"That is what has been bothering me," Sarah whispered.

"What is that, Sarah?" I asked.

"They take wood for the sacrifice, but no sacrifice. What does Abraham plan to sacrifice? No!" She crumpled to the ground in tears. "Not Isaac. Please, Jehovah, not Isaac."

Yael and Dorit, her new maids, helped me lift her to her feet and support her to her bed. She lay crying for much of the morning, refusing to eat or drink. In our concern for her, we brought her food and wine, but she refused. I sent Dorit to bring Refaela.

After examining her, Refaela shook her head. "Abraham and Isaac's leaving have brought her great sorrow. You need to encourage her to do something while she waits."

I nodded. "Is she strong enough?"

Refaela tucked her healing supplies back into her basket. "She is, if she chooses. It is your responsibility to help her choose life. Abraham and Isaac will need her when they return."

I watched Rafaela walk away before returning to Sarah.

"Sarah? Sarah," I whispered. "You must live for them."

"I know. But ..."

"You must do something. Show Jehovah your great faith. You are the most faithful woman I know. He will protect Isaac."

Sarah sat up and wiped her tears. "Isaac will need a blanket for his wedding night. He will find a wife in the coming years. I will weave him a blanket. Yael, Dorit, go home to your mothers. I will call for you when Abraham returns."

The other maids frowned. "They will want to know why you sent us home," Dorit said.

"I am well. But I will be busy. I would send Keturah home as well, if she had a mother to return to."

"You are my mother," I murmured.

Sarah nodded and shooed the other maids away. "Enjoy your mothers. Find a man."

Dorit and Yael scurried out the tent door.

I held Sarah's arm as she slowly made her way into the weaving tent. "What colors will you use?"

She stared at the dyed yarn in the baskets that surrounded her. "The colors of the desert. He will love it."

I helped her string the weft threads on her loom and sat nearby to retrieve the colors she needed. As she wove, her lips moved in prayer, begging Jehovah to bring her Isaac home to her. "But if you must take him," she continued in her whispered prayer, "I will submit to your will."

Bara and Liora brought her food, although she ignored it as she wove. I spooned it into her mouth. "You must eat, Sarah. Food will give you the strength to weave."

She sighed and took the bowl from me. "I will eat, but I must complete this blanket before Abraham and Isaac return."

When Liora returned to retrieve her bowl, she chided Sarah. "You must rest. You are not as strong as you once were."

"If I do not work, I will not finish Isaac's wedding blanket," Sarah would say.

Liora shook her head and left the weaving tent after watching her weave.

Sarah wove most of the day for four days. I convinced her to rest in her bed only because it became too dark to weave after the sun set. On the morning of the fifth day, she stood in the door of her tent gazing down the trail leading to Mount Moriah.

"What do you seek?" I asked.

"Perhaps Abraham and Isaac will return today," she murmured.

We stood watching for an time. Then she sighed and turned. "I will not finish Isaac's blanket this way."

I held onto her arm, holding her upright as we returned to the weaving tent. I flipped the tent door up so light would pour in onto her work. She spent the rest of the day weaving. I sat nearby, carding or spinning wool.

We spent time each of the next two mornings staring down the trail. Then Sarah would shake herself, put her hand on my elbow, and shuffle back to the weaving tent.

"If I am to make his marriage blanket, I need to finish weaving the fabric," she said as she sat in front of her loom.

I took my seat and spun the wool into thread.

On the morning of the seventh day, we sat together, Sarah weaving and me spinning. She clipped the last thread, and I stood to help her take the blanket from the loom when we heard a shout of welcome and Liora rushed into the weaving tent.

"Mistress! They have returned," she cried.

Liora and I helped Sarah stand and creep to the tent door. My eyes quickly found both Abraham and Isaac. "They both return," I whispered.

Sarah sank to the ground in a prayer of thanksgiving.

Isaac hurried to the tent and knelt beside his mother. "Are you well?"

"I am well and you are here," she replied. "I am thanking Jehovah for your return."

I stepped away from them while young men helped Abraham off his donkey and helped him hurry to Sarah.

I turned to find the other maids. We would be needed to help with meals and other things soon. As I walked away, I heard Abraham say, "All is well, my Sarah. I promised I would return with our son."

I brushed the sudden tears from my face. I did not expect to see Isaac again. It was a miracle.

Sarah told me later of Jehovah's command to sacrifice Isaac. I think Isaac knew, though he would admit only that he suspected he was the sacrifice.

"When Abraham had Isaac bound on the altar, and raised his knife to strike him dead, an angel stopped his arm, telling him not to slay the lad," Sarah told me.

"What did they sacrifice?" I asked. "Certainly there was a sacrifice."

"There was. They looked where the angel pointed and found a ram caught in a thicket. They used the ram as sacrifice in place of Isaac. Jehovah told Abraham he could now be certain of his trust and loyalty, for he would not withhold his son, even his only son, from Jehovah."

I shivered at the words. Such great faith!

"You knew. You were warned of it in a dream," I said.

"I did. And I knew Jehovah would provide us with many children. He returned Isaac to me. He loves me. He will bless us with children who will bless all the nations of the earth."

I let out a sigh. "What a magnificent blessing."

"It is. I am grateful I lived long enough to see the blessing begin. Isaac will have children, and his children will have children, and on and on."

Sarah's health continued to decline. She asked me to tuck the blanket into a trunk where I could find it when Isaac married. "You will need to spread it across his marriage bed," she said.

"You will do that," I said.

"No. I will not be here when Isaac marries." She slid down into the bed.

I feared she would not be long for this world. She spent much of her time reading the books written by the ancient matriarchs, especially focusing on the book Eve wrote.

Abraham sent for Refaela, who could only offer ways to help Sarah rest comfortably. "I cannot heal this illness," she stated. "I can only help to keep her comfortable."

Abraham brought her stacks of vellum, pen and ink, and a table she could set across her legs, admonishing her to write her story.

"Abraham asked me to do as Eve once did," she told me as I sat beside her, waiting to assist her with some small need. "He thinks the story of my life would help other women. I do not see how, since Jehovah insisted I wait so long to have my one child."

"We will learn of your patience and faith," I said. "Few women would patiently wait so many years for a child. Fewer would have allowed their husbands to take that only son to be sacrificed."

"I did what was required of me. I would not have chosen the things that happened to me." Sarah lifted her pen, dipped it in the ink, and wrote. After a few strokes of her pen, she lifted her head. "I hope others will also learn that Jehovah keeps his promises. Nothing is impossible for Him."

I nodded. "Truly. I have seen that with you and Abraham. I pray that some of those promises settle on me as your servant and maid."

Sarah's gentle smile warmed my heart. "I am certain they will."

I sat near her, carding and spinning wool, waiting for her to ask for water or food. I watched her stop to cough until I feared she could not stop. At first, the cough was small, only hindering her slightly. However, as the days passed, her cough became worse, causing her to stop for longer each time to regain her breath.

I tried to hide my concerns. My prayers for her health were constant as I watched her work. How would Abraham live without his Sarah?

I knew Abraham had sent messengers seeking news of his family in Harran, as he often did. A few months after his return with Isaac, he met some of these messengers in the hills above the village. He brought the news to Sarah's bed. I learned later that his brother had a granddaughter, a woman he could trust to worship Jehovah and marry Isaac.

I had cared for Isaac in a sisterly manner since Sarah brought me to her home. I never expected Abraham to consider me as a wife for his son. I had a soiled past, though Abraham never blamed me for the things Shet did to me. I could not be the one to give Isaac children.

After Abraham brought Sarah word of a woman in Harran, Sarah's cough slowed her writing and interfered with her sleep. I saw her wipe her lips after a coughing spell. Pink blood stained the cloth. My heart dropped.

"Abraham, do you know how ill Sarah is?" I asked when he came to sit with her while she slept.

He bent his head and a tear dripped onto his tunic. "I have seen the pink on her cloth after she coughs. Refaela tells me she has not long to live. What will I do without her?"

"You will continue to live, obeying Jehovah in all you do," I said.

He sucked in a deep breath and slowly let it out. "I will have no other choice. I would wish to go with her, but it is not yet my time. Someone must ensure that Isaac is married to a good woman."

"Isaac needs your strength," I agreed.

The next afternoon, Sarah handed me her pen. "I am finished. I have nothing more to say."

"Are you certain?" I asked.

She shook her head and a deep grating cough overcame her. "If not, I have no more energy to add more. I pray Jehovah takes me soon."

I fell to the floor beside her and grasped her hand. "Oh Sarah. I do not want you to die. You are more of a mother to me than my own mother. I have not missed Orpah in the years she has been gone. I cannot say that about you. I will miss you."

She squeezed my hand weakly. "I have no more strength to carry on. I have one thing to ask you, though."

"Ask me. I will do anything you ask." I never expected to hear her next words. I gazed into her eyes, waiting for her request.

"Marry Abraham and take care of him when I am gone."

My head jerked back. "Abraham?"

"I know you will bless his life and he needs someone to care for him. You love him."

"As a daughter, as a servant loves her master."

"But you love him. He will not do well without a wife. Promise me, if he asks, say yes."

She is giving me a way out. Abraham is old. He will not ask. How will I have children if I marry such an old man? Can I truly live with him? He is a hundred years older than me!

I nodded dumbly. "I promise. If he asks, I will marry him."

Death

Sarah died during the night a few days later, before Abraham could send a messenger to Harran to bring home a wife for Isaac. I stood at the edge of the tent, hoping not to be seen as she breathed her last words to Abraham and Isaac.

"Do not forget, Abraham. You promised."

Promised? What did he promise? Knowing Abraham, he would remember.

"I will send Amir in the morning. He will bring a wife for Isaac."

"And the other?" Sarah wheezed.

"Yes, and the other. I will do as you ask."

Not just Isaac. What else had she asked? Did she ask him to marry me? Could I say yes? I had promised Sarah I would. Had she trapped me?

I thought of Ezra, tall, strong, and young. During the years, he had not stopped coming at night to ensure I was safe. *Does he care for me?* He never said. *What will I tell Ezra if he asked me to marry him? He has not asked for my hand. Perhaps I am hoping for something that will not happen.*

"Isaac?" Sarah croaked softly.

Her son knelt beside his father and leaned close to hear her words. She spoke so softly, I only heard, "... wife ... Harran ... Jehovah."

"Yes, Mother. I will do as you ask." Isaac loved his mother and would obey her last request. She had spent many days worrying that he would take a wife from among the Canaanites who surrounded us, fearing he would lose his rights to the covenant made with his father. I knew he would wait for the messenger to return.

"Give my tent to Isaac," Sarah whispered. "You will not want it after I am gone."

Abraham lay his gray head beside her white one. "You know I will. How can I use this tent with all the memories we shared here? I would spend my days in tears."

Sarah lifted her head to gaze at Isaac. "Isaac may have this tent, when he brings a worthy wife to it, to make and share wonderful memories with her. I hope theirs are as remarkable as ours have been."

"How could I do anything else, Mother?" Isaac whispered. "I will bring my wife here. We will live in this tent, making memories together."

Tears dripped unheeded off my chin. I was losing the only mother who loved me.

She said something I could not hear.

Abraham lifted his head and spoke to me. "Keturah," he said. "She wants to talk to you."

I dashed the tears from my face. "Me?"

"Yes, you. Come quickly."

I hurried to Sarah's side and gently lifted her hand to my cheek. "I am here, Sarah."

"You will miss me, but remember, we will see each other again."

"Will we? Are you certain?" I glanced up at Abraham. He would know.

He nodded. My eyes returned to Sarah.

"I love you as the daughter I never had. Never forget that. But you do not need any of my possessions. You will receive a greater blessing when you marry Abraham."

I gulped and refused to look at him.

"Jehovah has promised me you will receive the children my body could not carry. You will provide children for Abraham. Bless his life and you will be blessed. Remember, I love you both." She tugged weakly on my hand and brought it to rest in Abraham's hand. "You will both be happier. This is all I can do to help bless your lives."

I stared into Abraham's face, but he did not look up at me. His eyes focused on Sarah, the love of his life.

"Once more, you give your maid to me. I want only to remember you."

"You may remember me, but marry Keturah. You need one who loves you to care for you."

"Do you love me?" His eyes lifted to mine.

Do I?

"I love you as I love Sarah."

"You will learn to love me as a husband, but not yet."

Sarah made a soft sound. We all turned to her and watched her breathe her last breath. She lay still after that, no longer moving, not breathing, not living.

Abraham touched her throat, searching for life. When he found none, he fell on her chest and sobbed. Sarah had lived 127 years.

During the night, Abraham and Isaac mourned for Sarah. I mourned for her in my quiet way, not as publicly as Abraham and Isaac. Tears leaked from my eyes as I prepared food for Abraham and cleaned Sarah's tent. I needed it to be clean when the rest of the village came in to pay their respects.

Abraham and Isaac took Sarah's body to Refaela to prepare for her burial, then he mounted his white stallion and rode west with some of his men. I feared for him, but he was not my husband.

I prepared the tent for the return of Sarah's body. When others stopped by to offer concern and sympathy, they often asked where Abraham planned to bury her.

"I do not know? I did not hear Abraham say anything about that. Perhaps that is where he went," I answered each time one questioned me.

I spent the day in prayer, asking that Sarah be kept in Jehovah's hands, and that Abraham and Isaac be blessed with safety and comfort.

Isaac entered the tent with a long, narrow bed, which he set up in the middle of the sitting room area.

"We will put Mother here when Refaela has completed her ministrations. There is no need for the villagers to tromp into her bedroom to pay their respects."

I nodded my agreement and found a blanket to drape across the bed and a pillow to rest her head on. Isaac searched through her clothing until he found Sarah's favorite dress.

"She will like that you chose that dress for her to wear," I said.

He nodded, tears threatening to fall on the dress. "I hope she knows I love her."

"She does."

My eyes turned west each time I heard horses, but Abraham did not return until almost night. He wearily slid out of his saddle and marched toward Refaela's healing tent. Isaac hurried to follow him.

When they came out, they carried Sarah's body between them, bringing her to her tent and setting her on the bed in the sitting room. I lit candles and rush lights so Sarah would not be in the dark.

Abraham and Isaac sat on either side of Sarah's body while the villagers came in to share their grief with them. I sat in the corner, watching each person enter. I thought of all the times Sarah had been good to me. There were so many.

"You will miss Sarah too," Ezra said, jolting me out of my reverie.

"I will. She saved me from Mother and Shet."

"She has been like a mother to you." Ezra knelt next to me and spoke in soft tones.

"Much better than Orpah was."

"What will you do now she is gone?" Ezra asked.

I shrugged. "Keep this tent ready for Isaac and his new wife to use. Feed Abraham. Help keep his tent clean."

"Isaac has found a wife?"

"Abraham will send a messenger to Harran to his brother's family. I expect he will bring a woman back for Isaac to marry."

"It is time Isaac marries. He is almost forty years old. Men should be married and have children before they are forty."

"What about you, Ezra?" I lifted my eyes to his. "You are not many years behind him, and you are not yet married."

"I have waited for my woman to be free. Are you free yet?"

"Me?" My heart thumped heavily in my chest.

"I have always loved you. Why do you think I have waited all these years? I have waited for you to be free."

"I have been Sarah's maid. She has not owned me. Did you not see that all her other maids have found husbands? She encouraged us to find a man to marry."

"Yet you have not." Ezra's voice carried pain.

"Not yet."

"Not yet?"

I traced the design woven into my skirt. "No man has asked me yet."

"Yet?" Ezra glanced around the room, seeking the man who would ask me. "That will change."

"Will you ask me?" I allowed my eyelashes to flutter as I had seen other girls do when trying to entice a man.

"I have wanted to ask you since before you left your mother's tent."

"Why did you not?"

"You were young, too young to marry. Then, Abraham and Sarah were your guardians. How could I ask Abraham for permission to marry you?" His eyes pled with me to understand.

"I fear it is too late now," I whispered. I cleared my throat. "You should have asked earlier."

"Why do you say that?" Ezra's rough voice made me shiver.

"I cannot say now, not now. Not until after Sarah's burial. But she has asked me to care for Abraham."

"You can care for him as my wife." His voice wavered with emotion.

"You have not asked me yet."

"This is not the place to ask you. But I will anyway. Keturah, will you marry me?"

Tears filled my eyes. "If only you had asked me a month ago. I have promised Sarah."

His voice became husky. "Promised Sarah? Promised her what?"

"That I would marry Abraham."

Ezra stalked away, hurt filling every step.

I did not want to hurt him. I did not want to tell him. But I had promised Sarah. Why had he not asked me earlier?

Burial

The next days were spent preparing to bury Sarah. Men packed our traveling tents onto the camels. Isaac and Abraham gently set Sarah's body into the bed of a small cart pulled by a donkey. They walked on either side of the cart. The rest of the villagers followed on foot, honoring Sarah.

It took us two days to walk from our current camp to the cave Abraham had purchased from Heth and his sons.

The cave was dry. A good place to leave a body. Abraham and Isaac gently carried Sarah's body inside and laid it on a rocky shelf.

"When it is my time," Abraham told Isaac, "I want to be laid beside her. She is the love of my life."

"It will be so," Isaac replied.

And me? What of me? Will you marry me and leave me for Sarah when you die? What will become of me?

A warm feeling filled my body and a voice whispered in my ear. "You will be blessed if you take Abraham as your husband. You will have children, and your sons will be blessed. They will share in the blessings of Abraham. You will be cared for."

I bowed my head and offered a silent prayer of gratitude. Jehovah had heard my concerns and given me hope. I would miss Ezra's strong, gentle hands, but I had committed to Sarah, as had Abraham.

Isaac assisted Abraham in building an altar on which they offered sacrifice. I sat near the back of the crowd, watching and remembering. I would miss Sarah.

Ezra stayed far from me. When I saw him, his glance appeared angry. What could I do? I had promised Sarah. Would Abraham keep his vow to her?

When we returned to our camp, Abraham moved my tent closer to his new tent. It was not as large as the tent he and Sarah had lived in. I was responsible for preparing his meals and keeping his tent clean, much as I had before Sarah's death.

He did not like eating alone. "Sit down and eat with me," he said at each meal.

I tried to avoid it, but he overcame my wariness, insisting that I join him.

"What if others see me eating with you?" I asked, chewing on my lip.

"They will have to think what they will. I do not like to eat alone and you agreed with Sarah that you would care for me. You must spend time with me if you are to learn that."

My face heated. I had not expected his attention to be so forthright.

I sat heavily in the seat and dished up food onto Abraham's plate, then filled mine. That first meal was strained. Abraham was almost as ill at ease as me. He asked questions about my day and sat waiting for me to answer.

I swallowed the food I put in my mouth before he asked and answered. "And ... and you, Abraham? How was your day?"

"Difficult." He rolled his lips inward. "I miss my Sarah."

I nodded and wiped away a tear. "I miss her too. Certainly, I cannot miss her like you do, but she treated me like a daughter more than a servant."

"She treated you much better than she treated Hagar, especially after she gave Hagar to me as a concubine. They developed a jealousy for each other. Sarah, because she could not give me the child Hagar did, while Hagar's jealousy came from my love for Sarah. I tried to treat them equally, but Sarah had been my wife for nearly seventy years. How could I not prefer her over Hagar?"

I sucked in a deep breath. "Are you certain Sarah was right about asking us to marry?"

Abraham leaned his head on his fist. "I do not know. There will be no jealousy between you and Sarah. But I will always love her. Can you live with that?"

"I would expect you to continue loving her. You were together for more than a hundred years. How can I compete with that?"

"You will not need to compete with Sarah. I will not marry you until my grief at her loss has lessened. Her loss left a hole in my life, a physical hurt. I cannot ask you to become my wife until I can say her name without anguish. Can you wait that long?" He took my hand in his. It warmed me.

"I can wait. I struggle to believe you would take me, a young woman, as your wife, rather than one of the older women. They could care for you and feed you as well as I can."

"They cannot give me children. Jehovah promised many children to me. Hagar gave me Ishmael, Sarah gave me Isaac. Two is not many." His face lit up. "Jehovah has told me you can give me more sons and maybe even a few daughters." The momentary joy floated from his face like the high clouds above us.

"Sons? Daughters?" I whispered. I had not considered ever having children. "Jehovah told you?"

Abraham nodded. "He did, when He confirmed Sarah's request. But He told me I could wait a short time, but not long. I am not getting any younger." His smile lit his face. I could see why Sarah loved him.

Each meal, Abraham requested we eat together. With each meal, we grew to understand each other better. His smile came more often and stayed longer.

"I have sent Amir to Harran," he said one morning. "He will bring us a wife for Isaac."

"Does Isaac know?"

He ducked his head. "Not yet. Amir left soon after Sarah's burial. I have not seen Isaac for two days. He went to Gerar to market our wool. When he returns, I will tell him."

"He should know before Amir returns with a wife for him," I said, leaning on my fist. "It would not be nice for a woman to discover her husband-to-be isn't expecting her."

Abraham nodded. "I will tell him as soon as he returns. You are correct. He will need to have time to be prepared for a wife. He has lived many years without a woman in his life."

Isaac returned three days later. Abraham invited him to join us for the evening meal, asking me to support him in telling him of the woman coming.

"I have news for you, Isaac," Abraham said after the food had been served.

"Oh?" Isaac lifted a bite of food to his mouth. "What news?"

Abraham filled his spoon with food. "You remember what your mother had me vow?"

"You would marry Keturah?" He stuck his spoonful of food into his mouth.

"You heard her ask that?" I asked, holding a spoonful of food in my hand.

Isaac swallowed his food. "Yes. She thought she was keeping her request private, but I stood close to them. I heard."

"And it does not bother you?" I set the spoon back in my bowl.

Isaac glanced up from his food. "Why should I be bothered by that? It is up to you and Father. You are the ones who will have to live with each other."

Abraham cleared his throat. "Yes, that, too. But your mother insisted that I send a messenger to Harran where my brother's family lives to find you a wife. You cannot marry a Canaanite woman, and you must marry."

"And you sent someone?" Isaac asked.

Abraham glanced at me. "I told you he is intelligent." He turned toward Isaac. "Yes. I sent Amir this morning. He promised to find Nahor and his family and bring one of his daughters or granddaughters to be your wife."

"Do you think he will can?" Isaac leaned forward and his face brightened.

"Amir vowed he would not return until he met with my family. He is a good man. I expect him to return with a wife."

"How long do you expect Amir to be gone?" I asked.

"When do you expect him to return?" Isaac asked, echoing my concern.

"Harran is a month's travel away. He left three days ago. I expect him to return no sooner than two months from now, probably longer, as he will have to spend time in Harran finding Nahor and his family and convincing them to spare a daughter or granddaughter." Abraham lifted his spoon and emptied it into his mouth.

"Two months, maybe more, before I may see my bride," Isaac mused. "I have much to do to prepare. Keturah, will Mother's tent be ready for her that soon?"

"It is ready now, unless you wish me to remove your mother's possessions. I keep it clean all the time." I did not tell him about the marriage blanket. He would see that for himself soon enough.

"No," both Isaac and Abraham cried.

"Leave Sarah's possessions there, except her clothing. Perhaps there are women within the village who need clothing?" Abraham said.

"What about Keturah?" Isaac asked. "Will she require new clothing when she becomes your wife?"

"I have clothing," I protested. "I am smaller than Sarah. Her clothing will not fit me." *How can I wear her clothing? Sarah was Abraham's wife. I would look like I want to be her, not myself, as I marry Abraham.* "It is best to find women who can use her clothing. I do not think your bride will want to wear your mother's clothing. I do not. I would feel strange wearing her clothing."

"I suspected you would not want to wear her clothing. After we are married, I will provide you with more clothing, clothing to indicate your status as my wife, no more as a servant or maid."

"Will the people accept me?" I had spent many days since Sarah's burial worrying that I would not be accepted.

"They will. It is my right to marry whom I will. I am the leader of this village. How can these people argue with me?"

"They may not argue with you, but they will grumble among themselves," Isaac said. "I have heard them when they think I am not listening."

Abraham shrugged. "They will do what they do. I cannot stop them. However, you must prepare yourself for a bride."

"What must I do?" Isaac asked.

"I sent jewels and silks for her and her family. You must be prepared to receive her."

Isaac ducked his head, thinking.

I glanced at Abraham, who winked at me.

When Isaac lifted his head, he smiled and stood from the table. "Thank you, Father. I have waited many years for you to find me a wife. I look forward to Amir's return."

Abraham stood and clapped Isaac's shoulder. "It is past time for you to wed. Perhaps I will wed soon after, but you must be married first."

"Why?" Isaac asked.

My thoughts echoed his question.

"I must give no appearance of dishonoring Sarah."

"She insisted you marry Keturah," Isaac spluttered.

"Our people were not with me when she exacted that commitment from me. They do not know, nor will they understand. I must continue to grieve in public, as I will always grieve in private." He took my hand. "I will never dishonor you, Keturah, but Sarah was my first love."

Proposal

Amir seemed to take forever to return. After two months of waiting, Isaac wore a path between his tent and the fields closest to Harran. He wanted to be there to welcome his bride away from the prying eyes of the men and women of our village.

I understood. As I walked to the well, I was often stopped along the way as women asked about what would happen to our community.

"What will Abraham do now?"

"When will Isaac take a wife?"

"Why has Abraham left Sarah's tent empty?"

"Does Abraham not still love Sarah?"

"Why are you still helping Abraham?"

And many other questions I had no answer for, and had no desire to share the answers I had. The women were curious and concerned, for the answers to those questions would affect their lives.

I told them I continued to help Abraham because Sarah asked me to. As for the other questions, I could not answer. I was but a servant.

But am I just a servant? Abraham speaks of our marriage. Sarah extracted a promise from both of us to marry. Does that make me his servant still? What would Isaac do if Amir did not return with a woman for him to marry? I never expressed that fear, though I saw it on Abraham's face occasionally.

Two months and ten days after Isaac learned of Amir's journey, he trekked to the fields once more, hoping to see the woman who would be his wife before the others. The jingling of camel bells echoed in the distance. Amir must have returned.

I returned to Sarah's tent. I found the blanket she had so lovingly made for Isaac and spread it across the big bed. Isaac and his new wife would sleep beneath it as she had dreamed. I dusted everything one last time, leaving the tent door open to air out any mustiness. After today, it would no longer be my duty. It would be the duty of Isaac's new wife. As I finished, I looked around, remembering the good things that happened to me in this tent. After that day, I would no longer be able to return and breathe the memories of Sarah. It would belong to another woman, creating memories for Isaac and his new wife.

I heard the shouts of young boys accompanying Isaac and the woman who would be his wife. I slipped out of the tent and returned to mine. The tent was now hers.

I heard Isaac calling to Abraham. "She is here, Father, and she is beautiful. Come, you must meet her."

I heard their voices as they passed by my tent once more. Isaac's wife was here. How much longer before Abraham declared his choice to marry me? Would he ask me or assume I would uphold the promise I made to Sarah? Or had I misunderstood him? Would he follow through with his promise? I paced within the confines of my little tent until my stomach gurgled with hunger.

Abraham would still need food, as would Isaac and his new bride.

I hurried to the cooking fire and checked the food I had started earlier that morning. I called Yael and Dorit to help me serve them. Yael nodded and agreed to come help, while Dorit tittered. "Isaac finally has a wife. I wondered how long it would take him."

"It took as long as it did. Abraham charged him with a promise he would never marry a Canaanite woman," I said. "We must ensure their first night together is memorable."

"We can do little to help with that," Yael said, with a grin and shake of her head.

"No, but we can provide excellent tasting food."

We completed the preparations, then the three of us carried the food to Sarah's tent. I would always think of it as hers, even though another woman would now occupy it.

I scratched at the door when we arrived, and a strange woman opened it with a questioning gaze.

"We bring a wedding feast for the master and his new bride," I said.

The woman stood aside while we carried in the food and served Isaac and the tall, beautiful woman who sat at the table with him. Amir had chosen wisely, if looks meant anything. After serving them, we set the extra food on the side table and left. The stranger followed us.

"I am Deborah," she said. "I have been Rebekah's nurse since her birth. She does not need me now."

Dorit giggled.

"Is there a place for me to stay? Amir took the other girls who came with us somewhere. I stayed with Rebekah until after her formal marriage."

"Amir took them?" I asked.

"I saw him with strangers earlier," Yael said. "I know where he took them. I will show you the way. Certainly, he has a place for you to stay as well."

Yael and Deborah walked away, visiting softly.

"A new mistress," Dorit said. "I did not expect Isaac to find such a beautiful woman."

"She is beautiful," I agreed. "Amir did well in finding a wife for Isaac."

"I must return to my husband," Dorit said. "Thank you for asking me to help."

"I knew I could trust you," I said.

"Always," Dorit said, and turned on her heel and hurried toward her home tent.

I stood in the path, staring after her. A new mistress? I suppose Rebekah was. What would they say if I married Abraham?

Abraham! I whirled around and rushed up the path to his tent. He would need food as well.

I dished up his food and carried it into his tent.

"You took food to Isaac and Rebekah?" he asked.

"I did. They needed a feast. Are they married?"

Abraham sat at his small table and motioned for me to join him. "Rebekah's father, Bethuel, insisted on a vicarious marriage before she left home. He said it would keep her safe on the journey. I did not consider that before sending Amir off. Bethuel is still a wise man."

"So Isaac was married and did not know it?" I asked as I passed him the roasted mutton.

"He was. But I performed the rite once more, so both he and Rebekah could respond. Rebekah needed to hear Isaac's answer, and Isaac needed to hear the rite, and Rebekah's answer." He passed the meat back to me and took the tubers.

"That makes sense. Who witnessed the ceremony?" I dished meat and vegetables onto my plate and handed the vegetables to Abraham.

"Her nurse, Deborah. She is a lovely woman."

"I met her. She is a pleasant woman, if a bit austere." I handed the bread to Abraham to slice.

He chuckled. "Perhaps."

We talked about Rebekah and Isaac as we ate. Then, before I cleared away the dishes, Abraham spoke again.

"Isaac will be happy with Rebekah, although he did not know her before today. We have known each other for a few years. Will you marry me? I believe we can be happy together."

Tears leaked from my eyes. "You will honor the promise you made to Sarah?"

"Yes. I will treat you well. We can find joy together. Will you fulfill your promise and marry me?"

"I am much younger than you. I could be the daughter of your daughter."

"Young enough we can have many children together. Are you willing?"

"If you are certain, yes. I am willing."

Abraham took me by the hand and pulled me from my chair into an embrace. "I suppose we should not be alone together until our marriage," he murmured into my ear.

"We have been alone together all this time. Will it matter?" I whispered.

He leaned back. "It matters to me and it matters to Jehovah. I will eat near the cooking fire until our marriage."

I looked into his eyes. I saw affection there. Perhaps, in time, love would come.

Marriage

We did not see Isaac or Rebekah for the next two days. We probably would not have seen them then, but it was the Sabbath. Although she stood straight, Rebekah clung to Isaac's arm as they entered the sanctuary. She stood a bit shorter than Isaac, but not by much. I did not remember she was so tall, but she had been sitting when I saw her.

I wondered how I would react as the newest woman in Mamre, and the wife of the leader's son. Probably as she did, uncomfortable. Had she ever been away from her parents? It must be hard for her. She relaxed some during Abraham's teaching and leaned her shoulder against Isaac's.

I would be patient with her. I doubted she would remember me. How could she, as her attention had been on Isaac?

After Abraham's declaration on the night of Isaac's and Rebekah's wedding, I struggled to keep my focus on his words. He was old, past one hundred thirty years, and I had not passed my thirtieth year. I remembered before he took Isaac to be sacrificed. We all feared he would not live. Yet now he stood straight in front of the assembled group and spoke of treating others with respect, as Jehovah would.

As I left the sanctuary, I heard people talking about accepting Isaac's new wife.

"She is quiet."

"But she is beautiful."

"We must help her, be her friend."

"Find ways to serve her. It must be hard to be so far away from her home."

"She seems a bit pretentious."

"She seems frightened. It must be difficult for her to leave home to marry a man she doesn't know."

I agreed. Life for Rebekah would be difficult until she got to know the women of Mamre. I wanted to help, but the other women saw me as a maid, a servant, not a woman of importance. How would that change when Abraham announced his intentions to marry me?

I stayed busy, keeping Abraham's home tent clean and cooking for him, as I had since Sarah's death. When I had nothing else to do, I carded and spun wool into yarn. I had not woven often, although I had watched Sarah. I knew I could do it when given the opportunity. Would I have the time and opportunity to weave? Sarah's loom still stood in her weaving tent close to her home tent. I did not have a loom or space to put one.

I searched through my clothing for something appropriate to wear on the day Abraham would marry me. At the bottom of one chest, I found the blue dress Avi gave me when Mother and Shet left me behind. I put it in my chest, thinking I would wear it later. It had several straps that were difficult to tie. Because of this, I had not worn it. Now would be a good time, but how would I get it fastened?

Two days after the following Sabbath, Abraham invited me to join him one afternoon when Isaac brought Rebekah to visit. I sat in the chair near Abraham, as he requested. I knew what he planned to say, but I feared Rebekah's response.

"I have asked Keturah to be my wife," Abraham said. He took my hand. "She has agreed."

Rebekah stepped forward and embraced me. "Congratulations, Keturah. We will be family."

"It will be good to have family again," I agreed. "I have not had a family since my mother left Mamre with her new husband." Rebekah did not need to hear all the details.

"You did not go with your mother?"

"Her husband did not want me and Sarah needed me. So I stayed." A simple response would do. My stomach clenched at the memory of Shet. *Would he never leave me?*

Abraham and Isaac moved to one side of the tent and discussed the words Isaac would use when he performed our marriage rite. Rebekah and I moved to another part of the tent where we visited.

"How can I help you?" Rebekah asked.

"I have a special dress I would like to wear, but it is difficult to put on. Would you help me?"

"I would love to. I have a wedding veil —"

"No. I am Abraham's third wife. Some may consider me a concubine. I do not deserve the veil."

"Every woman deserves a wedding veil!" Rebekah cried.

"No. The marriage rite will be simple, after the Sabbath service. I do not want to bring attention to myself."

"You are the bride! One of us should get that attention."

"You have the attention, as Isaac's bride. I will get more than enough attention as Abraham's bride. How can I, a young woman and the maid of his past wife, marry Abraham, who is old and the leader of our community? I have no status, no parents, no wealth. What can I bring him?"

"Your love, your caring, and your attention," Rebekah replied. "What more can a man wish from his wife?"

"Children."

Rebekah snorted, and we giggled together until Abraham and Isaac joined us.

"You two sound happy," Isaac said, pulling Rebekah close.

"We are. We were discussing what would keep our men happy."

"Food, good food," Abraham said as he put his arm around me. "We always love food."

Rebekah and I glanced at each other and laughed.

"What did I say?" Abraham asked, his eyes wide.

"It is a woman thing, I think," Isaac said.

The following Sabbath, Rebekah came to my small tent to help me dress in the blue dress Avi gave me years before. With her help, it fit. She lifted flowers from a basket.

"I brought flowers for your head, since you will not wear the wedding veil."

"They are beautiful, but I do not want others staring at me during Abraham's teaching. It is enough that I am wearing this rather than my usual dress."

"You always look beautiful," Rebekah said, returning the flowers to her basket. "I will bring the flowers with me and set them on your head before Isaac performs the marriage rite."

I closed my eyes, swallowing the tears that wanted to drip down my face. "I always wanted my marriage day to be special."

"I know," Rebekah replied. "I did as well."

As a little girl, I thought Mother would help me with a special dress and make me a wedding veil. Then she married Shet. After they left, I hoped perhaps Ezra would ask to marry me, and Sarah would help me dress. How things changed from those past dreams. Never in all my dreams did I think or hope to marry Abraham.

"But yours was even more simple, with few witnesses."

"Only Deborah, here. I was married to Isaac before we met. Father insisted we marry vicariously before I left home. He said it was to protect me on the road. I think he wanted to see me as a bride."

"I hear fathers are like that."

We walked together to the sanctuary tent, where Isaac wrapped his arm around Rebekah. "I missed you," he whispered.

Would Abraham miss me?

I settled into a seat next to Rebekah and turned my attention to Abraham, who shared a message about the love of Jehovah and all his many blessings. My legs bounced and my stomach was filled with jitters, making it difficult to focus on his words. Would he actually marry me?

Then it happened. Abraham stopped speaking and looked out into the crowd, then gestured for me to come forward. I stood, but before I could walk to stand beside him, Rebekah reached into her basket and lifted the flowers out. She gently placed them on my head.

"I am lonely without Sarah," Abraham said. "Keturah has helped me with my needs, but I want her to be my wife. Isaac will perform the marriage rite for us." He signaled for Isaac to come forward.

People behind me murmured softly. Some did not seem surprised.

Abraham took my hands and we stood together, facing Isaac. He said the words he and Abraham had discussed earlier. When he spoke of bringing children into the world, I glanced sideways at Abraham, who grinned.

Food? Men want more than food. They want children.

Isaac pronounced us husband and wife, and suggested Abraham kiss me. I swallowed my fears as Abraham took me in his arms. That first kiss was intense. I knew he wanted me.

When it ended, the crowd sighed. Abraham took me by the hand, and we walked out of the sanctuary to a new tent.

"What is this?" I asked.

"My tent is small, like yours. I asked Isaac to purchase us a new and bigger one. You deserve a tent fit for the wife of the leader."

I walked around the tent, touching the new chairs and tables. "We will gather other possessions to fill it. But for now, simple is good," Abraham said.

He led me to the bedroom. New blankets spread across the enormous bed. Along the walls were chests and trunks, including the trunks from my tent. "I had my men bring your trunks here after you left. I want you to be comfortable.

He took me in his arms and kissed me again, taking my breath away. How could a man as old as him have the strength to kiss me like that? But he did.

And his loving afterward was gentle, yet powerful. I no longer feared he would not be able to be a good husband.

Listening

"We stayed in our tent for three days. Women left food outside our door. When we hungered, I retrieved it, and we ate.

At the end of the three days, we held hands and walked together into the sunshine. We greeted the men and women we saw. They offered us congratulations on our marriage. Abraham had warned me this would happen, and I held my head high and accepted their kind words with the grace he expected.

"Do you weave?" he asked.

"Sarah taught me to weave, but I never had a loom to use."

"I will fix that. A woman should make the fabrics she desires."

"And the blankets and rugs."

"Yes," Abraham nodded. "Those too. Sarah enjoyed creating with her loom. If you prefer another way of creating, I will support that."

"I have had little opportunity to consider creating anything beyond a meal and a clean home."

"That will change. You need maids."

"Maids?" I cried. "I know how to care for my home."

"But you are now my wife. When men come to trade, I need to show my wealth and power."

"Your animals show that, do they not?"

"They do. But my wife cannot be tied to washing our clothing, cleaning our home, and cooking our food. You will need time to sit with me in conferences. Find three young women who need help. Consider maids as your opportunity to help young women who may struggle without you."

"Like Sarah helped me?"

"Yes. You were recommended to her as a hardworking young woman, but your struggles with your mother and Shet led Sarah to believe you needed her help as much as she needed yours."

I ducked my head. "She gave me much more help than I could ever repay."

Abraham lifted my chin. "Do the same for others. There are young women who need to be needed. Find them. We can provide them with more than work. Perhaps give them a small coin each week."

"Or their parents," I murmured.

"Yes, or their parents." He waved to one of the men walking past. "You can do this."

I smiled. I appreciated his support. Yes. I could help other young women as Sarah had helped me.

We walked a distance before I spoke again. "Do you have any suggestions?"

"I trust your judgment. You will find girls who need your help. Keep your eyes and ears open as you walk through Mamre. Listen. You will find the right ones."

Listen. I could do that.

We stopped by Isaac and Rebekah's tent. It seemed odd to enter their tent and see everything moved and rearranged. I wanted to cry out, 'That is not how Sarah would have things,' but I knew the home no longer belonged to Sarah. It was now Rebekah's.

"You look well," Isaac said.

"I am," Abraham replied. "And does not my bride look exquisite?"

I wiggled my toes in the soft carpets. *Me? Exquisite? No one had ever suggested that for me. Other descriptions, perhaps, but never exquisite.*

"I think she does," Rebekah said. "I thought she was beautiful before, but now she glows."

"Beautiful? Me?" I shook my head. "I am not beautiful."

"Ah, but you are," Abraham said. "Sarah could see it beneath all your pain when you first came to us. I think that is why she kept you so close to her."

"Because I was hurting?" The flush of my face increased. I could not tell if I was more embarrassed or indignant.

Abraham wrapped his arms around me. "Beautiful, dear. She knew she would not live long. She knew I would need another wife. She kept you close for me."

My eyes widened. "All the years I was her maid, she planned to give me to you, as she gave Hagar to you?"

"No, not as she gave Hagar to me. This time, she gave us both the privilege of deciding for ourselves. She asked me to promise I would marry you, but only after she saw we would be happy together."

"She asked me to promise her I would marry you if you asked. I agreed, never expecting it would happen."

"She knew your inner beauty and grace. She knew you were the woman for me. But she did not force it on us. You are my wife, not a concubine, as Hagar was." He kissed me gently.

"I thank her for that," I said, shivering at the joy of his kiss. *He cared for me. Perhaps he would learn to love me. Maybe our love would not be as intense as his love for Sarah, but it would be right for us.*

I enjoyed caring for Abraham's needs, but he was right, as always. I needed a maid or two to help when he entertained others. As I walked through our village, I watched for young women who needed succor, support, or relief. At the well, as the women discussed their lives, I listened.

"Ada is growing. I am uncertain what to do with her," Aliya, her mother, said one day.

"Does she run around with the young men?" a friend asked.

"Yes. She does not know how to stay home. I fear for her chastity. She is becoming wild."

Ada.

I put her name in my mind, deciding I would pray about it.

"Young women today seem to struggle," another woman said. "My Shifra has problems as well. She is not chasing into the hills after the young men, but she struggles to find meaningful activities to take up her time. I often find her sitting and staring into nothing."

"My daughters did that," another woman said. "They settled down after a few months. It helped that Refaela needed an assistant and asked Lila to help her. The others soon found young men who married them. That always settles a girl."

Shifra. Two young women who could use help. Ada and Shifra.

"Did you teach your daughters to cook and clean?" Galia asked.

Both mothers looked offended. "Of course we did," Ada's mother said.

"What kind of mothers do you think we are?" Shifra's mother cried.

"We all teach our daughters those things," Lila's mother said.

Each mother sounded outraged that Galia would ask. I wanted to hug her for asking, so I did not need to ask. If I had asked, they would have been angry with me.

I will pray about these girls. Father will help me decide.

I took my turn filling my water jug from the well.

"Keturah," Shifra's mother said. "We did not see you waiting. We should have allowed you to go first.

"Why?" I asked.

"You are Abraham's wife. You have better things to do than to wait for a turn to draw water." Ada's mother said.

"But I enjoy listening to you. I have never been a mother. It is good for me to hear about your challenges."

"You are not ..." Ada's mother stuttered.

"Not, what? With child? Not yet. I have only been married to Abraham for a few weeks."

"You would not be the first to find herself with child soon after her marriage," a woman said, touching her growing stomach.

"You did, did you not, Kyla?" a woman asked. "And look at you, with child again, with two little ones at home. Where are your little ones?" the woman looked around for little children.

"Yes, my Joshua came near the end of the first year of our marriage. And Luna came much sooner than we expected after Joshua."

"Three little ones?" I asked. "And all young?"

Kyla gazed at me and stood taller. "Yes. My man has strong seed."

My face reddened. "I did not intend a lack of courtesy."

The women laughed.

"Kyla is easily frustrated." Her friend stuck her tongue out at Kyla. They giggled together. "She is with child again. It is hard on her to have three children in less than three years."

"Three in three years? I am sorry."

Kyla tipped her head back and guffawed. "You have no idea, Keturah. If Abraham's seed is as strong as my man's, you will find out."

I sucked in a deep breath. "Could that happen? He is old."

"It could," Galia said. "Women become too old, but men do not."

"Oh." I picked up my water and walked away. I had so much to think of. Girls to ask to be my maids and children.

As I walked home, Abraham joined me and took the water jar from my shoulder.

"Let me carry that for you."

"I am able," I protested.

"But you should not have to carry it. Did you learn anything?"

I shared the things I learned about young women at the well with Abraham. I did not share the teasing about children. Was it true?

Could old men give their women children as often as young men? Abraham had only given his women two children.

"You should pray about it before you decide," Abraham suggested.

"I struggled in ways these girls have no way of knowing," I said.

"Your mother's husband was a horrible man."

We reached our tent. I directed Abraham to set our water jar inside the tent where it was cool.

"He was. I do not believe these girls have men like that in their lives."

"I certainly hope not. If they do, those men will be sent from our village." His sudden anger surprised me.

I put my arms around him. "You did the right thing for me. You saved me from Shet." I kissed him.

"And I will save any other girl who faces the things you did." His voice softened. "You have grown much in the years since then."

"In many ways."

Abraham lifted me from the floor and carried me into our bedroom. "We should see if my seed is as strong as Hyim's is."

"Who?"

"Kyla's husband. I heard what she said." He kissed me again.

I leaned back and stared at him. "How?"

"I heard her bragging. I waited until you were away from the well before I caught up with you."

"They say older men can father children."

"I have heard we can. Shall we see?"

New Maids

After praying. I decided to give Ada the opportunity to work for me. I found her mother and spoke with her.

"I am here to invite your daughter to become my maid. I have cared for us, but Abraham recommends I need maids to help when he has guests. Would Ada work for me?"

"I would lose her help. As my oldest daughter, I depend on her to help in our home and with her brothers and sisters."

"Yes. But we will offer you a farthing to make up for your loss of her time."

"Farthing? How many?"

"One a week."

Her eyes opened wide with greed. "That much? I expected much less. Ada gives me much less help than that. I will take one every other week."

"You do not value her enough," I said.

"You do not know her. If you continue to use her help after a week, I will be surprised."

I raised my eyebrows. "You think so little of your daughter?" *Was this woman like my own mother, grasping and greedy?*

"No. I know her. She runs off to avoid work. You will see."

"I will see, and so will you. Where is she? I would like her to begin now."

Ada's mother turned and shouted. "Ada. Get out here now. Someone wants to speak to you."

I cringed. I did not expect a screaming mother. I could understand why the girl ran to get away.

Ada stepped out of the family tent with hair tangled and wearing a dirty dress she obviously threw on, rubbing her eyes with dirty fists. If she were smaller, I would think she was three, not thirteen.

"What do you want?" she snarled. Her eyes widened, and her snarl softened when she saw me.

"I came to offer you a position as my maid. Abraham thinks I need help keeping our home clean and food cooked. You know how to do those things?" I peered into her face, hoping to see into her soul.

She bobbed her head. "My mother taught me how to do those things, although she does not remember I can do them well without being nagged."

"She said she had taught you. That is why I considered you." My gaze followed the lines of her disheveled body. "How long will it take you to make yourself presentable?"

"You would have me be your maid?" Ada's eyes opened wide as she unconsciously shrunk back a step. She ran her fingers through her hair.

"I would. Can you be ready in half a span?"

Ada glanced at her mother, who frowned at her. "Yes. You can go with Keturah."

"Yes," Ada said, backing toward the tent. "I can be ready sooner than that."

She dashed into the tent. I sat on a rock that outlined the paths to wait. Her mother returned to her work, cleaning wool to prepare it for spinning.

"You do a good job cleaning the wool," I said, attempting to engage her in conversation.

"I have to if I want to make a good trade," she grumbled.

"We all have to do our best work if we want to make good trades. I learned that long ago."

She mumbled something I could not hear or understand. I shrugged and lifted my head toward the morning sun. The warm rays on my face felt good.

"You will get brown skin if you do that," Ada's mother warned.

"Yes, if I sit in the sun for a long time. But I will not be here long. Ada will join me soon."

"You think better of her than I do."

"I have learned to give people an opportunity to show the best of themselves. Until I learn otherwise, I treat them as if they are at their best."

"Ha! Ada will teach you otherwise."

"We shall see." I leaned back and closed my eyes. The sun felt lovely on my face.

"Shall we go?" Ada asked, much sooner than the half span I gave her.

I looked up to see a clean, lovely young woman. "Yes. I think we should. Ada will return after dinner. We will feed her, so do not wait for her."

Together, we walked down the path toward my new home.

"Did you mean what you said to Mother?" Ada asked.

"What did you hear?"

She kicked a stone down the path. "That you give people the opportunity to prove themselves to you and treat them as if they always do their best?"

I reached the stone and kicked it down the path. "Yes. I believe that. Sarah taught me many things. She taught me that the most important thing I can do for myself is to expect others to do their best. People live up to my expectations. I expect you to be an excellent maid."

"I do not know how to be a maid, excellent or terrible." She kicked the stone farther than before.

"I was Sarah's maid. I will teach you." I turned and smiled at her. "You know the basics. I will teach you what I would like done and how. You are a fast learner. You will serve us well."

"Us?" Ada squeaked.

"Abraham lives with me, as you know. As you serve me, you will serve him."

"Oh." Her body sagged.

"He is an honorable man. He treated me with kindness and courtesy when I served Sarah as her maid. You have nothing to worry about."

"But he is the leader of our village," she said, shrinking into herself.

"And he will treat you kindly as he does all the other members of our village."

I watched her out of the corner of my eye as Ada considered my words. She rolled her shoulders back and stood straighter.

We walked up the path to my tent. "Come. I will show you what I need first."

Ada worked hard. She stayed until long past our evening meal before returning to her mother's home and returned early the next morning.

At the end of the first week, I gave her two farthings. "Give your mother one of these. The other is for you. She said you were not worth a coin. I disagree. You are worth many more."

Ada's eyes opened wide. "One of these is for me?"

I nodded. "Tuck it away where your parents and brothers and sisters cannot find it. You worked hard for this. You do not want to lose it."

"How did you know they would take them from me?" She chewed on her lip.

"I had parents and brothers like yours. I had to hide my coins from them."

She grinned and tucked her coin into her shoe. "They will not find them here."

"Remember to take them out of your shoe and hide them when no one is around."

Ada grinned. "You know I will. I will see you tomorrow?"

"No, tomorrow is the Sabbath. We rest on the Sabbath. Enjoy your day. I will see you early on the morning of the next day."

When I asked Shifra's mother for her daughter to help me, she was much more positive and grasping.

"Shifra is a good girl. She is a great help to me. I will miss her working beside me. She works hard and it will be difficult for me to lose her." The woman's eyes glinted with greed.

"I can help some with that. I will give you a farthing every other week to make up for taking her from your home," I said, knowing it would not be enough.

"I hear you offered Ada's mother a coin every week to replace the work her daughter did for her."

"And she refused it. It would not be fair to her for me to give you more than I give Ada's mother."

"My daughter does more for me than hers did for her."

I sucked in a breath. I did not want to give her the coins. "Perhaps I will have to find another girl to help me."

I turned to walk away. "I thought Shifra would be a good addition to my household. I guess I will not find out."

I stepped away, almost to the end of the path leading to their tent home.

"I will accept a farthing every other week," Shifra's mother said.

"And you will not ask for more?" I stared into her face. "You agree to my payment?"

The woman stared at me for a long breath before she sighed. "Yes. I will accept your terms. But once you see how valuable she is to you, I would not argue if you give me more."

"No doubt. We will see. Do not expect it anytime soon. Is Shifra here?"

"I will call her. She is washing our clothing."

I nodded and sat on the large rock at the entrance to her path.

"Would you like to sit here?" the mother asked, indicating a chair.

"No, thank you. I prefer to sit out here where I can feel the warmth of the sun. Will you get Shifra?"

Shifra's mother strode off around the tent, returning soon with her daughter. Shifra's hands and face were red from the heat of the wash water. Her hair was tied up on her head. She wore older clothing, as I often did when washing clothes. She dried her hands as she came around the tent.

"Mother says you want to speak to me?" she said, dipping her head.

"I came to offer you a position as my maid. Are you wiling to work as hard for me as you do for your mother?"

"You cannot possibly ask me to work as hard as my mother." She turned her head to see if she had been heard. When she saw we were alone, she continued. "Mother loves to keep me busy all day. She fears I will get into trouble if I am not working."

I nodded. "My mother thought much the same, but I believe young women need time to sit and think. Do you read and write?"

"No." Her face fell.

"I thought not."

"Will that keep me from working for you?" Shifra sagged.

"We can change that. But first, go put on better clothing. You will serve Abraham and me. You do not want to be dressed in the older clothing you use for washing clothes."

Shifra glanced down at her dress. "I have one dress that is better. I will put it on."

"Only one? I will change that."

But Shifra had already hurried into the tent. I offered a silent prayer of thanks to Jehovah. I had found two girls who would need my help. I only needed one more.

I no longer went to the well for water, as Ada and Shifra did that for me. However, I still needed one more maid. So I walked through the village at odd times of the day, listening to mothers, to daughters. After three weeks, I wondered if there was another girl for me.

I prayed for assistance. Then I asked Shifra and Ada if they knew a girl who would appreciate coming to help me.

"We know of lots of girls who would like to work for you," Shifra said. "They think it will be easier for them to find a man to marry if they are working for you."

"Some think they can find a man from among those who visit Abraham," Ada added.

"They would have a Canaanite man?" The thought shocked me. "Do they not remember the love of Jehovah?"

"Those girls are vain and prideful. They do not care about you. They want your farthings and a chance to meet young men."

"Those are not the girls I desire." I set my head in my hands and shook it. "How am I to find a girl who will serve me, one I can help?"

"Is that what you are looking for?" Ada asked. "I wondered why you came to Mother that day. You have changed my life. She cannot scream at me all day if I am not there. And if she screams at me in the evening, I find a reason to come back here to help you."

"I wondered why you were out by the cooking fire in the evenings after you should have gone home."

Ada shrugged. "I would rather sit by the fire here than go home to be screamed at. Mother does not understand."

"No. She does not."

"And I am not exhausted when the day ends," Shifra said. "You keep us busy and we work hard, but not as hard as Mother worked me. And I love that you teach us to read and write."

"Do you know another who would appreciate what I have to offer? Not the coins, but the reading and writing and ..." I spread my hands wide, "this?"

The girls thought, then almost together they said, "Tamar."

"Her father was injured in a hunting accident last year. He is grumpy and demanding," Shifra said.

"And her mother requires her to stay at home to help with the children while she gathers wool and works in the fields. We seldom see her at the well or anywhere the girls gather anymore."

"Are there other girls at home who can help with the younger children?" I asked. I could not take her mother's only helper.

"She has an older sister who escapes to the fields," Ada said.

"And a sister who is only a year younger than her. They could help with the other children."

"Chana is often sad, as well. Her mother has too many children and depends on her to clean and cook. When she comes to the well, she has little to say. You may think of her," Ada said.

"It sounds like her mother needs her."

"She has brothers and a sister just younger than her."

I nodded. "I will take this to Jehovah and Abraham. Thank you for the suggestions."

After the girls went home that evening, I spoke to Abraham about the girls Ada and Shifra suggested.

"I cannot take a girl who is needed from her family, but you said I should choose one who needs me. Both of these girls sound like they could use my help."

Abraham took my hand in his and squeezed. "You have a good heart, Keturah. Take this to Jehovah."

"And if He says to choose both girls, can we give both parents a farthing?"

Abraham grinned. "Coins are not the concern. We are concerned about helping girls and their families. Jehovah will guide you. If He suggests you choose both girls, do it."

After praying, I took a walk. As I passed Chana's home, her mother sat in front of their tent, fanning herself and her stomach, swollen with a child.

I sat in a seat near her and visited, learning that Chana had many duties in her home, more than any of her sisters.

"Do you have other daughters who can take her place?" I asked.

"Why? She is my oldest. It is her responsibility to care for her younger brothers and sisters."

"I have need of another maid. The young women who help me suggested Chana."

Her mother snorted. "She is much too busy here to waste her time in your home."

"I understand that. Would it not help her next younger sister to take some of the load? Would it not help that daughter prepare for her future? You want your daughters to find husbands and give your grandchildren, do you not?"

She started to spit out a response, but stopped. "Bina is a beautiful girl. The men will love her. She will bring us a large bride price. But she will need to know how to care for a home and children. Perhaps she should share the responsibility."

Another grasping, greedy woman. Why are our women so selfish?

"Bina is a beautiful girl, as is Chana. If Chana becomes my maid, she will bring a greater bride price."

"But who will teach Bina?" the woman whined.

"Who taught Chana?"

"I did, but I am great with child."

I inhaled a slow, deep breath to calm myself and said a silent prayer to Jehovah. "Perhaps Chana has taught Bina while you were sleeping?"

"Perhaps." She glanced toward the back of the tent. "Chana insists her sisters help her with washing the clothing. Bina knows how to do that. But can she cook or clean?"

"She will need it if a husband will keep her."

The mother slowly nodded her head.

"And," I added, knowing it would tip my hand, "I pay the mother a farthing every other week to make up for the services of her daughter. Could you use that?"

Greed glittered in her eyes. "Every other week?"

"Until she is of marriageable age."

Chana's mother bit her lip as she calculated. "A coin would help. When would you want Chana to begin?"

"Today?"

"I need to be certain Bina can take over. Can you wait until after the Sabbath?"

I sighed. I wanted to bring her to my home sooner, away from the grinding press of her mother's requirements. "I suppose I can wait."

"And will you take Bina later?"

"It depends. I may not need a maid when Bina is old enough."

"Then another of my daughters?"

"I will think about it. I will make no promises. For now, I would like Chana to come to my tent this evening after your evening meal."

"She must clean up the dishes."

"Bina can do it. She will do it when Chana is with me."

I stood to leave. "Do not forget to tell her I expect her this evening."

"She will be there," Chana's mother called. "When will I receive the coins?"

I stopped. "After she has worked for me for two weeks." *No need to pay before she has worked.*

I found Tamar's mother in the fields. "How is your husband? I asked when she stopped for a break.

"His leg causes him great pain." She frowned at the thought.

"That must be horrible," I said, trying to allow concern to fill my voice. "Are you able to provide enough food for your family?"

"If I spend every day helping in the fields or gathering wool. It is a constant struggle."

"What can we do to help you? Your life cannot be easy."

She sighed. "No, but I cannot take charity. Shemer would be angry."

"Will he heal?"

"Refaela does not know. She thought his leg would have healed by now. She wonders ..., I cannot say it. It would not be fair to him."

"I need another girl to help, especially when Abraham invites his trading partners to come here. It has become easier for him to trade from here than to travel to their homes. Would it help if I brought Tamar into my home as my maid? I would like her to join us."

"Why would you do that?" Tamar's mother asked. "She is a girl."

"And the right age to be my maid. I can teach her to do things as I prefer. Your ways are wonderful," I said, before she could become indignant. "But we each have our ways of doing things. I am certain you have taught her well."

Tamar's mother shook her head. "I have not been home for a year to help teach her. It will be a blessing for you to help her. She will learn better out of Shemer's grim view. He is less than patient with her."

"Will two farthings a month make it easier for you to spend a little more time with your children?"

"Two farthings a month?" Her eyes shone with unshed tears. "They would make a big difference. I miss working with my children."

"I will talk to Abraham about —"

"Please do not. It would offend Shemer."

"I will be careful. Men understand the pride of other men. Abraham may know how Shemer can be more productive and find greater hope and pride in himself. Abraham will say nothing to Shemer about us talking."

"It would be a relief for our family if he could."

I nodded. Shet had become more irate as he depended more on Mother than on his own efforts.

"When can I expect Tamar?"

Tamar's mother bit her lip. "Could she come to your tent this evening, after we eat and clean up?"

I nodded. "That will work. I will see her then."

Feast

Tamar and Chana were soon integral to the running of our home. I wondered how I had managed our home alone. I could do it again, if I needed to, but I enjoyed their company.

It was not long before Abraham had guests from other lands visit. The girls helped clean the tent and prepare a feast for the guests. Abraham would not allow me to help serve.

"You are my wife, not my servant," he said. "Your purpose is to be at my side, looking beautiful. We have four girls who are able to serve us."

"Are they able? Do we trust them?"

"You have taught them well. They will be fine."

After the conclusion of business, I sat beside Abraham at the feast where the men celebrated the new contracts. Abraham's sheep and goats provided the best wool in the area, and men paid high prices to obtain it.

The men enjoyed the food and wine we provided. Everything went well until, as the girls cleared the plates from the table, I heard a pile of plates crash to the ground, shattering.

Tamar shrieked and fell to the ground near the end of the table, trying to gather up the broken earthenware. Tears flowed down her face as Ada and Chana hurried to help while Shifra ran to get a basket for the chunks and shards.

"Go to them," Abraham encouraged.

I joined them, bending to pick up the largest pieces of plate near me.

"What happened?" I asked.

Tamar sniffed. "He touched me." She nodded toward the young man who sat at the end of the table.

"Touched you? How? Where?" I asked.

She rolled her lips inward and wiped away the tears. "He put his hand up my skirt and touched me here." She touched her bottom.

"I am sorry, Mistress," she cried. "I should not have reacted so. But I have never had a man touch me like that. It startled me."

"No man should touch you in that way except your husband," I said. "Can you get this picked up? You and Ada?"

They nodded. Most of the mess was already cleaned up. "Shifra, you and Chana go get the dessert and start serving it. Take these men's minds off the broken plates."

The two girls jumped up and hurried toward our cooking area. "We will talk about this later," I said. Then I saw Tamar's face twist in fear. "But I am not angry with you. We will discuss how to deal with rude men."

I rose and walked as gracefully as possible back to my seat. "Dessert will be here soon," I said to the men who waited.

Abraham glanced at me. "What happened? Did she stumble?"

I turned toward him and put a hand in front of my face so others would not hear or read my words on my lips. "The young man on the end of the table by Tamar believed he had the right to touch her skin beneath her skirts. She has never been touched that way before. It startled her."

Abraham turned to briefly stare at the man. "I will resolve this, but not now. You can be certain that young man will never touch our maids improperly again."

"Do not cause Tamar undue grief. She is upset already."

"Oh, I will not," Abraham said. "I have dealt with this behavior before."

After the men left the table, Abraham put his arm around one of the buyers and walked with him a distance. The buyer's face grew scarlet as he listened to Abraham's words. He walked away from Abraham a distance, then returned and spoke to him once more.

Abraham returned to my side. "It will not happen again."

I lifted my eyebrows.

"I will tell you more later."

I walked to the serving area and found the girls cleaning the dishes. "You did a great job today. I am proud of you."

"Even though I broke many plates?" Tamar asked with a tear-stained face.

"It was not all your fault you dropped the plates. It is difficult when young men believe they have the freedom to touch the women who serve them. You are not required to accept their unwanted touches."

"What do we do, then?" Shifra asked. "He tried to touch me, but I moved away before he could."

"He was not the only one," Ada added. "A young man on the other side of the table tried to touch me."

"Which young man?"

"The one with a light beard and red hair. He acted like he was important," Ada said with a shudder.

"That one? I saw his rudeness. I did not see him try to touch you."

"He thought he could do it without being seen."

"Keep cleaning. We will discuss ways to stop inappropriate behavior later." I turned to leave, then saw Tamar's face twist in fear. "I do not hold you responsible for the broken dishes. We can replace them. Do not fear."

I wandered among the men who continued to stand visiting until I saw Abraham. He spoke with the red-haired young man. I grimaced and swallowed. Abraham needed to know.

I touched his arm.

"Keturah," he said. "How can I help you?"

"Can we speak?" I asked. "Alone?"

"A moment, if you please," he said to the young man and stepped back a few steps with me. "What is the problem?"

"That man you are speaking with ... Who is he?"

He turned his head to glance at him. "You mean Khaba?"

"Yes, the man with red hair."

"That is Khaba. Is there a problem?"

"He tried to touch Ada in ways he should not. Is this something your guests often do?"

"It is not. My guests know I do not accept such behavior. We protect our women here."

Khaba stepped toward us. "Is there a problem?"

Abraham rolled his shoulders back. "Yes, Khaba. There is a problem. Keturah is telling me you forgot the standards I set before you entered my camp. I protect *all* the women in my community. A woman who is serving us does not need to fear you touching or grabbing her. I told all of you I would not sell to men who take advantage of our women."

"Khaba stepped back. "I did noth—"

"Keturah reports you tried to touch our maid in an unacceptable manner. I cannot sell to you."

"But I ordered more wool than any other man," Khaba exclaimed.

"It does not matter," Abraham said in a low, even tone. "You will receive no wool from me."

"I paid!"

"And your gold will be returned to you. My women are not prey for your roaming fingers. I am sorry. I cannot sell to you."

"Cannot, or will not? Because I touched a girl?"

"That girl is my wife's maid. She is protected here."

"And what of Hu?" Khaba protested.

"He will receive no wool from me, either. His son broke the rules of my home. I warned you before you came here. I cannot change the rules for you or anyone else."

"I will ..."

"Receive your gold back and leave my village." He turned and signaled for Eliezer, his steward.

Eliezer hurried to his side. "Do you need some assistance?"

"Yes, Eliezer. Return Khaba's coins. He is leaving now."

Eliezer ducked his head. "If you will come with me, I will return your bag of gold." He turned and walked away, expecting Khaba to follow him.

Khaba's angry stare at Abraham concerned me. Then he spun on his heel and followed Eliezer.

"He is angry," I said with a shudder. "I have caused you to lose a sale."

"No, Keturah. You did not cause this. I would have discovered his dishonesty, eventually. He did this to himself."

"But the gold you are returning —?" I asked.

"— Will be replaced by another buyer. I have others who wanted more wool."

"Will they pay as much as Khaba?"

"It does not matter. Our women are more important than gold I may receive." Abraham hugged me. "Thank you for sharing this information with me. Now I have to meet with the others."

I nodded and walked back through the men. One stopped me.

"Did you say Khaba touched one of your maids?"

I bowed my head. "He did. I did not intend to cause him problems."

"He deserves to lose his purchase. Thank you. I will speak to Abraham. I need more wool."

The man strode off toward Abraham.

I returned to the serving area. "Abraham protects you. He sent the red-haired man away with his coins."

"He lost his sale?" Ada gasped.

"Khaba lost his purchase. Another man will purchase the wool he lost."

"That is good," Shifra said.

"Jehovah watches over us."

That night, Abraham held me close in his arms. "Thank you for warning me about those two men."

"It never happened when I served as Sarah's maid. Is it because you are so tough?"

"It is. This is not the first time I have rescinded a sale. Most of these men know my standards and that I refuse to sell to a man who abuses our women."

"I appreciate your protection. I did not know you were so careful of us."

"Sarah knew. That is why she could accept those men coming here. I went to their homes before, but I am too old to travel now. Men from around come to me, because they know I sell the best wool they can purchase. Because it is, they cannot purchase it from another."

"How often will this happen?"

"Every year after shearing, and sometimes during the year. It depends on if we sell all we produce in the first sale."

"And you always warn them of your proscription against touching women?"

"Always. That warning goes with every invitation." He pulled me closer to him. "I will invite Khaba and Hu to come again next year. Perhaps they learned I mean what I say. If not, they will not be invited back. Ever."

"That is harsh."

"The women here are more important than the gold I can get for some wool. I prefer the men of the lands around know my word can be trusted."

I kissed him. “I appreciate your care for us.”

“Jehovah cares for his daughters. How can I do any less?” He kissed me passionately and I melted into his arms.

A Child

The week after the feast, I woke with a queasy stomach. I had been sick before, but never like this. Only my stomach rebelled. I did not burn. Abraham had risen early and left me to sleep that morning. After a morning of losing anything I ate, I rose from my bed and began my daily chores.

That afternoon, when he returned, I sat in a chair, my head drooping in my hand. He rushed to me and knelt at my feet.

"What is wrong, my sweet?"

"I have struggled with my stomach all day. I do not know why. I am not ill, and I have eaten little today."

Abraham set his hand on my stomach. "Here?"

I nodded listlessly.

"And you have no vigor?"

"None. I have accomplished nothing today." My stomach rebelled again.

"How long has this been happening?" he asked.

I thought back. "I have been queasy for a few days, but today is the first day of total nausea. What is happening to me?"

Abraham got a cloth and dampened it. He wiped my forehead with it. "Does this help?"

I was surprised. "It does."

"You have not been around women who are with child, have you?" Abraham asked.

"My mother, but I was young, too young to know what was going on with her." Then his words made sense to me. "You think I carry a child?"

"We can hope you are. It would be lovely if you do. I would be happy to have more children."

Me with a child? Already? I did not believe it could happen. Certainly not this soon.

But as the days passed, the symptoms got worse. I carried a child. I admitted it to myself and to Abraham, who wrapped me in his arms.

"Jehovah has blessed us. You must take care of yourself."

"Why? I am a strong woman."

Abraham ran a finger along the side of my face. "You may not have any problems, but Sarah did."

I had heard rumors, but I had not believed it before. Not until Abraham told me.

"I am not Sarah. Many women have children and few lose their children early." I hoped I was not one of the few who lost their children early. "My mother had no problems. She had several children. I will probably be like my mother."

After several days of sickness, it slowed, and finally ended. We went to visit Isaac and Rebekah soon after. Abraham told them our news. I ducked my head, unsure how they would react. But Rebekah leapt forward to embrace me. "I am excited for you. Congratulations. How are you feeling?"

"It has been a difficult week, but I am feeling better now, I hope." I set my hand on my stomach.

"We will have to do something special for you and the baby," she gushed. "I will make a blanket for you and your child."

I thanked her. *Did I dare ask her to help me learn to weave?* "Could you help me learn to weave? I need to make clothing for the baby."

"You never learned to weave?" she asked.

My face burned. "My mother did not weave. After I became Sarah's maid, I helped with the wool, cleaning and carding before helping her to spin it. We always had wool to spin."

"Always. We constantly need wool and fabric. I would be happy to teach you."

After that, the sickness took me to my bed for a short time in the mornings, but not as long as that first week. As I became accustomed to having a child growing within me, I seldom became sick.

Rebekah wove a soft blanket for our baby. By then, I seldom suffered from the sickness. Abraham set up a small tent near ours and put in a new loom.

"This is for you," he said. "I hope you enjoy it."

As much as Sarah enjoyed hers. I swallowed the trickle of jealousy. *You know he loved her.* I scolded myself. *He loved her and took care of her for many years, more than a hundred. He has a right to think of her. He is trying to do for you what he did for her.*

I smiled. "I know I will. Rebekah said she would help me weave. I know some of the basics from watching Sarah, but Mother never wove. She did not teach me."

"How sad for you," Abraham said, putting his arms around me. He never missed an opportunity to show me his love. "You will learn. And if you do not love it as much as Sarah did, I will not mind. You are a different woman, with unique talents. I will still love you."

"Like Sarah," I said, "I love you. You are so good to me."

"I love you. Not in the same way I loved her. She was my first love, the love of my life." He ran his hands through my hair, brushing back a lock of hair that had fallen into my eyes. "You are the love of my old age. I love you differently, as you are a different woman. But I love you deeply. I did not think I could. Sarah was right. I needed another woman. I needed you." He touched my stomach. "And you are giving me a child already."

I felt clumsy as I strung the warp threads onto my new loom. I had watched Sarah many times, even helping her, but I had never done it alone. It took longer than I wanted, but they finally looked right. Rebekah came to my weaving tent as I finished, exclaiming at the threads and how even they were.

"It took me forever," I said. I heard the complaint in my voice and lifted a shoulder. "But I did it."

"You did. Do you have threads for making a blanket? Blankets are the most forgiving to weave as a first project. They can be uneven and loose and still provide the warmth you need."

I had a basket of yarns I had spun in the days since Sarah's death. They had not been dyed, but I liked their natural color. I pointed to it. "I have these."

She squatted next to the basket and examined the threads. "You have beautiful threads."

"Sarah taught us to spin almost as soon as I became her maid. My mother did not need to spin, since she did not weave. But I have been spinning and carding for many years now." I sighed. "I watched Sarah and sometimes helped her string her warp threads in her last years. She never thought to teach me to weave. That was her joy, her thinking time."

"I understand that," Rebekah said, standing with a hank of the yarn. "I do my best thinking while I weave. Here, let me show you how to begin. You have much experience watching. It is time now for you to do."

With significant patience, Rebekah guided my hands and taught me the intricate moves of weaving. We spent most of that morning together inside my weaving tent, and I had a good start on a blanket for the baby when she left.

One day, shortly after Rebekah taught me to weave, I sat with my four girls, working to teach them to read and write. None of their mothers had learned the skills.

Shifra looked up from her bark. "Mother thinks we waste our time learning to write and read. She says you must be crazy to teach these skills to me. If anyone should learn to write and read, it should be one of my brothers."

Like Sarah had done with me when I first came to her, I had started them drawing in the dust outside the door to our tent. When they had mastered the symbols we used for letters, we moved on to sheets of bark stripped from the sycamore trees. We used pens made of twigs blackened on one end.

Eventually, I would give them sheets of vellum. Vellum came from the skins and the process was long. I did not participate in creating vellum, but I knew it was not as easy to get as the strips of sycamore bark. Even I used sycamore bark to make notes for my household, until Abraham saw what I was doing and gave me a small book made of vellum to write on.

"Your mother does not have these skills?"

"No. None of my family can."

"Men should have this skill, but so should women. How can we keep track of our belongings? How can we remind ourselves of things we want to do? Or how can we know what others from far away may tell us in their messages?"

"Mother says those things should be kept in our memories. Messages can be read to us."

"This is true, but if a message is written, I can know for myself what the sender wanted to tell me. Most importantly, however, if I can read, I can read the sacred books that teach of Jehovah. I am not dependent on others to tell me what He taught ancient people."

"You have access to those books because Abraham has them," Ada said. "Most men do not have access to them."

"Abraham would allow others to read them if they ask," I said.

"Will he allow us to read them?" Chana asked. "I would like to read them."

"When you can read well enough," I answered.

"I heard there are books written by the matriarchs of old," Tamar said.

"There are. Sarah had a copy of the book Eve wrote. I read it."

"Was her life much different from ours?" Ada asked.

"In some ways. She was alone."

"Tell us some of her stories," Chana begged.

"After you have practiced reading and writing. I will talk to Rebekah. She has that book now. Abraham left all of Sarah's possessions in her tent and they now belong to Rebekah. Perhaps she will lend me the book Eve wrote so we can practice reading."

The young women spoke excitedly about what they thought was in Eve's book, then bent to practice their writing in earnest.

When they returned to their chores, I went to Rebekah's tent.

"Are you struggling with your weaving?" she asked when I entered.

"No. It is coming along well."

We talked about weaving for a time before I brought up books. "In the days when I was first with Sarah, she taught her maids to read and write."

"Those are important skills for women to have," Rebekah said. Her hands were busy spinning as we visited.

"I agree. So much so that I am teaching my maids the same skills. My young women will soon read well enough to read books written by others."

"That is good. What books will you have them read? We have so few."

"I know. We sometimes read from Eve's book. Sarah had a copy. May I borrow it from you?"

"Eve's book?" Rebekah asked. She rose and walked to a trunk. She opened it and moved things around in it before she returned. "Is this the book you need?"

I looked longingly at the book I had not seen since before Sarah's death. "That is the one."

"Here. It is yours." She handed it to me. "My mother sent her copy of a collection of all the early matriarch's books with me as a wedding gift. I do not need this extra copy of Eve's book. I give it to you as a wedding gift."

My eyes widened. "You would give it to me?"

She smiled her gentle smile. "I have copies of her book and the others. As Abraham's wife, this book should belong to you. If you would like, I will lend you my copy of the other books." She handed the book to me.

My hands trembled as I took it from her. "This is for me?"

"Yes. You need to have Eve's words close by. They will help you."

"I remember Sarah said they helped her. Thank you." I clutched the book to my chest. "When I came, I only hoped to borrow this book."

"And now it is yours."

My maids and I took turns reading from Eve's book. As they read, they grew more confident. We talked about the stories she told. Some were difficult for them to believe.

"How can you believe she lived in a world by herself?" Tamar asked.

"I believe the words of Adam. I have read from his book. Abraham allowed me to read it. I trust his words and the words of Jehovah," I said.

"No woman was there to help Eve," Ada cried as we read of her first time giving birth. "I am grateful we have Refaela to help you. Can you imagine only having Abraham to help your baby be born?"

The girls tittered at the thought.

"I can imagine it. If required, Abraham could do it," I said.

"At his age?" Chana asked. She opened and closed her mouth.

"At his age," I said. Inside, I was light and confident. He could do it.

The young women around me glanced at each other with wide-open eyes, then giggled.

I shook my head. "I am not saying I expect him to help me deliver this child," I said, setting my hand over where the child grew. "I am saying he could do it. I am grateful Refeala and Deborah are here to help me. Times have changed some since those first days."

"I think I am glad about that," Ada murmured.

"Me too," I said.

We all laughed together then. Abraham could do it if he had to, but why make him when there were women who had helped other women before? I was perfectly willing to trust Refeala and Deborah.

Rebekah had gone on a trading trip with Isaac and returned as my child grew within me. She came to join us in the afternoons, sewing clothing for the child and exchanging stories with me.

My maids sat near, helping to stitch clothing and listening to our stories. I sometimes saw their eyes widen as Rebekah spoke of helping Isaac with his trading.

"Mizran's eyes were shifty. He was up to no good," she said, regaling us with stories of her recent journey. "I warned Isaac to be careful. Mizran tried to get Isaac to sell it to him for less, much less. Then he tried to extort us."

"What did you do?" Chana asked, bringing her hand to her chest.

"Isaac told him we had more men surrounding him than he had in the dark little tavern. When Mizran took time to look, he realized our men filled much of the room, and they had weapons ready to protect Isaac and me. He tried to bluff us, but our men guarded us as we left the tavern. We found another buyer, who told us Mizran had locked him in a horse stall so he could steal from Isaac. He did not expect me to recognize the signs of his deceit."

"Isaac should take you with him all the time," I said. "Though I will miss you if you leave us every time he goes on a trading journey."

"He will take me some of the time. We talked about him being more watchful. I think he knew, but he let me think I was important."

"You are blessed to travel with him," I said. "I am happy to stay home with Abraham. He is happy to be with me and watch our child grow within me. It kicked last week. You should have seen his face when he first felt it. You would think he had never felt a child kick within his mother before."

I chattered about the babe and our hopes for him. I hoped it would be a son. Abraham needed more sons, but I wanted a daughter or two as well.

When Rebekah left, Shifra helped me clean up the mess while the others finished the evening meal.

"You should be more careful about your words," she murmured.

"Careful? How?" My eyebrows rose. *What had I said this time? I did not want to hurt others.*

"Did you not see the pain in Rebekah's eyes. She has not conceived a child. I saw pain cross her face as you talked of your babe."

"But she has not been married a year yet," I said. Sarah had waited many more years, and she often spoke of her pain. My heart twisted within me.

"Neither have you, yet you carry a child. I only say that she has sorrow within her because she is not yet carrying a child."

"I understand that. I heard Sarah speak of her pain. I did not think Rebekah knew the sorrow so soon." I lay a hand on Shifra's arm. "Thank you for seeing what I did not. I will be more careful of my words when Rebekah is here."

"She will appreciate that." Shifra smiled at me before cleaning up the rest of the dishes.

In the coming months and years, I minded my words as I watched Rebekah try to hide her grief at her childlessness.

They Climb

Over the next months, my body expanded bigger than I ever thought it could. The child within me moved and stretched, active often at night when I wanted to sleep. I would scoot my big stomach next to Abraham's back and let the child kick. How could I stop it? Abraham was amazed that I could sleep through the kicking. The babe kicked so much during the day, it did not matter. I adjusted to it.

Ada, Shifra, Chana, and Tamar joined me when I read to them from Eve's book. We often talked about how the world had changed and how it was still the same. My maids squealed at the delivery of Eve's first child and cried when the first children left Home Valley to follow the Destroyer.

"I see people who listen to the Destroyer still," Shifra said, dropping her spindle and allowing the threads to straighten. "My parents struggle with that. Mother asks every week for her coins. She would take mine if she knew I received coins as well."

"My father prefers to lie in his bed rather than do the work Abraham offers him," Tamar said. She carded the cleaned wool straight so it could be spun. "He likes having his wife and children provide for him, rather than doing what he can."

"I see others who struggle with listening to Jehovah," Ada said, spinning her thread. "Everyone struggles with the temptations of the Destroyer."

I would not share about Mother and Shet. It hurt to remember those days. What could I do to change them? Nothing.

"It is how we respond to temptations," Chana said. "My parents have had to learn that they will receive no more coins from you than those you agreed to. Mother wanted more. I hide mine from them."

Each of the girls nodded.

"My mother would not take mine, or I do not think she would," Shifra said, glancing at the other girls, then looking at me. "What she does not know will not hurt her. I have not told her of the coins you give me."

The other girls added words of agreement. They, too, kept the news of their growing stash of coins to themselves.

I nodded and rubbed the place on my stomach where the baby kicked. "It is wise of you not to share. If you need to help them, you will have many coins."

"What were your parents like, Keturah?" Ada asked. "We never hear you speak of them."

"No. I do not speak of them for a reason. They left me behind when they left. I chose not to go with them, for reasons of my own. They were not good people, much like the children of Eve who left Home Valley."

"And, like Eve," Shifra said," you wish they had followed the commandments of Jehovah more closely."

"You are correct. I do." I returned to reading to them from the book.

We stopped frequently to discuss the challenges of Eve's life and compared them to our challenges.

I went back often to chapters discussing Eve giving birth to her children, especially as I drew closer to the time of my child's birth. I wanted to know what to expect.

Abraham stayed close to home, in the last days when it was near to the time for the child to be born. He wanted to be with me when it was time.

After reading about Eve's experiences, I asked Abraham to give me a blessing similar to the one Adam gave Eve. He had me sit in a chair and stood behind me, placing his hands on my head. I felt a warm tingle rush through my body as he began to speak, sharing Jehovah's words with me. I knew those words came from Jehovah.

From Abraham's words, I knew Jehovah loved me. I stopped fearing the experience. I was as prepared as I could be.

Early one morning soon after Abraham's blessing, I woke with cramping in my stomach. The cramping increased in intensity and came back often. By the time Abraham woke, the cramps came so close together I struggled to breathe between them.

"Why did you not wake me?" Abraham cried when his eyes opened and he saw me puffing out breaths to control the pain.

"You were sleeping. You need your sleep," I said, sucking in another breath and rubbing my stomach as I puffed out the air.

"Not as much as you need Deborah and Refaela." He rose from the bed faster than I had ever seen him move and hurried out the tent door.

I continued to breathe and rub the spot on my belly where it cramped. I did not have time to worry about Abraham or the healers. All I could focus on was the cramping that had become pain.

Refaela rushed into our sleeping space, calling out orders to Abraham and my maids, who had somehow appeared. She threw back my blanket and pushed my legs apart and probed me in places only Abraham had touched before.

"How have you waited this long?" she gasped. She turned toward the sleeping room door and called to my maids. "We need hot water, now, and clean cloths! This baby is on his way!"

Baby? On the way? Is it time for the child to be born? Is this what it feels like?

Refaela stepped close to me and touched my face to get my attention. "Your baby is coming. I need you to take a deep breath and push the baby out."

Push the baby out? How?

I took a deep breath and pushed down.

"That is the way, Keturah," Refaela said to me. "Push, push, push," she called until the pain lessened. "Good. Rest until the next pain."

Abraham grabbed my hand and squeezed it. "You are doing well. The baby will be born soon."

I moaned as he wiped the sweat from my forehead.

"Soon, dear Keturah," he murmured, his voice soft and loving.

My stomach tightened again and I took another deep breath.

"Push!" Refaela called.

"You can do this," Deborah said.

When did she come? The thought flitted through my mind, then the pain intensified and all I could think of again was pushing the child out of me.

"Stop!" Deborah said, her voice commanding.

"Stop?" I gasped. "Stop what?"

"Do not push for a bit. We need to move the child so he can come out. Pant, if you must, but do not push."

I nodded. The need to push was great, but I did not. Instead, I panted through the pain while Refaela and Deborah did something to the child.

"Push on the next pain," Refaela called again. "The babe will be out in one or two more pains."

One or two more? I only want one more!

I pushed as hard and as long as I could until I felt something slip from within me.

"You can stop and rest now," Abraham said, dabbing my forehead. "Our child is born."

"Born?" I asked.

"He is born."

"A boy?"

"We have a son." Tears filled his eyes. "Thank you, Keturah. You have given me another son."

After they did more to me and the child, Deborah lay him in my arms. "Here is your son. Congratulations."

I cradled the little boy in my arms. This tiny child had lived within me. Abraham leaned close to look into the babe's eyes. The little one stared up at him with wide open brown eyes. Abraham ran a finger along his little face, then turned his eyes to mine. "He is beautiful."

I nodded. We had a baby boy.

We named him Zimran.

Isaac was excited to have a brother, even if there were more than thirty years between them. He was a beautiful child, with long limbs and dark hair and eyes. We all loved him.

It did not take him long to crawl sooner than I ever wanted him to. I loved snuggling with him during the day, but he soon wanted to be on the floor where he could explore. I learned to put away things I wanted to keep out of his reach. It did not take long for him to pull himself up to the baskets and trunks to explore what was in or on them. I had to ensure the trunks could not be opened and keep only items that were safe for him in the baskets. It meant I had to rearrange everything to protect our home and our child.

Dara and the other mothers laughed when I complained. "We have all been required to move our possessions out of the reach of children," she said. "Wait until he begins to climb. Then what will you do?"

"Climb?" I cried. "Children climb?"

"Do you not remember your brothers? I am certain they climbed on things in your mother's home."

I thought back. It had been many years since she left, and more since I spent much time in her tent with my little brothers. "They did, but not often. She had little for them to climb on."

"You left her home while you were young. Eleven, if I remember right."

"Yes. I was eleven. I have spent most of my life with Sarah and Abraham. I miss her. I am grateful she asked Abraham to marry me."

"Who would have thought that skinny little girl would become wife of Abraham, with all the blessings you have as his wife?" Daara asked.

"I never did. I liked Ezra then."

"Ezra?" Deborah asked. "Do I know an Ezra?"

"The herder. He married Degana when he heard Abraham would marry me. I think he hoped I would become his wife, but," I shrugged, "he never asked. Sarah and Abraham did."

"Her little boy is two weeks younger than Zimran," Tamar mused as she helped me put special trinkets into a trunk. "It is sad you have to hide all these pretty things."

"It does not surprise me. Ezra is a good man. He will be a good husband and father." I set a book in the open trunk. "I would rather have these hidden away in a trunk than torn or chewed on by a curious little boy."

We worked together to make our space safe for our child and safe from his grasping little hands. I would miss seeing the objects we hid in the trunks, but I knew where they were, and Zimran would not be a child forever.

Little did I know, for I carried another child soon after Zimran was weaned.

Isaac loved his little brother and carried him on his shoulders. He took him into the fields to see the growing grains and up into the hills to see the goats and sheep. He and Rebekah took him into their home when the sickness of carrying a child forced me into my bed once more.

Even after the birth of our first daughter, little Eila, Isaac took Zimran with him, teaching him of growing plants and animals. Zimran would return from a day with his brother, excitedly spewing all the things he learned that day.

I appreciated Isaac's help, for Abraham rarely went into the fields or climbed the hills to be with the animals. However, he still loved his horses and often took little Zimran to the paddock where he kept his horses. He would have his white stallion saddled and lift the boy onto the saddle before climbing on behind him.

Zimran squealed with delight. He loved the horses as much as Abraham did. Abraham gave him a pony for the celebration of his fourth naming day.

After thar, Zimran rode around the village and often into the hills with the herders. Ezra brought him home one evening. "This little man is learning to be a herder. The sheep have become familiar with his pony, and today as he sat on his pony he saw a wolf sneaking up on the new little lambs. Zimran cried out, and we were able to chase it off before it could take a lamb."

Zimran glowed at the praise.

After that, he went to the hills as often as I would allow him. All the herders watched out for him. He learned to care for the animals and grew stronger every day, as all Abraham's sons did.

I gave birth to four more boys, Jokshan, Medan, Midian, and Isbak, and three girls, Eila, Anath, and Nogahh. Our tent filled with joyful noise as children laughed and played together. The noise and children often spilled out of our tent into the surrounding land. We were a happy family.

Hagar's Death

Abraham's age caused him to move more slowly in the twenty years we had been together, but not as slowly as he had before Sarah's death. He had lived many decades. Even so, once again I found myself with child.

As always, Abraham was tender and protective of me. I reminded him of my strength. Although I had lost no children, he remembered the early days with Sarah and feared I would lose this one. I continued my chores as always, knowing Jehovah would care for me.

Then one day, a messenger arrived from Ishmael. Hagar was ill and close to dying.

"You should go to her," I said. "You loved her, and Ishmael is also your son."

Abraham shoved his hair back from his face. "I loved her in my own way. She wanted me to love her as I loved Sarah, or as I love you. However, I could not. Sarah was my wife, and Isaac was my promised son. I could not leave them for Hagar and Ishmael."

I leaned against him. "Ishmael will need your strength in his time of sorrow."

"He is a strong man." His voice quavered.

"And he will need his father. Go to him. Hagar will want to see you once more before she dies." I gently nudged him with my shoulder.

"You would not care if I go see her?" He looked at me with a slightly dazed look.

I set my hand on my growing stomach. "Why would I mind? You love me. We have another child coming. I have proof of your love for me. She has only one son and you sent her away. She needs you now, as does Ishmael."

"It is strange that neither Sarah nor Hagar had more than the one son. You have five sons and three daughters."

I grinned at him. "Your seed is strong."

Two days later, he left with three servants. Isaac wanted to go along, but Abrahan insisted he was needed here to watch over our camp village and me. Isaac grumbled, but he stayed behind.

One day after Abraham left, I visited with Rebekah in her home.

"Are you not concerned with him going to see Hagar?" she asked.

"Why would I be concerned? Hagar is dying." I dropped my eyes to my lap. "Since Sarah gave Hagar to him, Abraham has loved her in his own way. He says not like he loved Sarah or the way he loves me, but he loves her. Before Sarah died, I saw him leave to meet with Ishmael's wife and perform their marriage rite. Sarah still loved Hagar and gladly sent her husband to see to her needs. How can I show any less grace and kindness? This will be the last time he travels to Paran. Even now, he is too old to travel so far."

Jehovah, bring Abraham safely back to me, I silently prayed.

"He has used a stick to support him and keep him upright since I first came here, but now he clings to it. Both his hands and the stick tremble."

I rolled my lips inward. I had seen the same thing. "His strength is failing him. His servants had to help him on his horse for the ride to Paran. I fear he will join Sarah sooner than I want."

Rebekah's arms surrounded me in a loving embrace. "Abraham loves you. He will be with you as long as Jehovah allows. You are blessed to have him as your husband."

"I am blessed. Abraham has shown me great love."

In the weeks before Abraham's return from Paran, I struggled with concern for him and his health. I looked for his return each day after the first week. I knew he would not return so soon, but I watched the trail from Paran each morning and evening. My eyes strayed to the trail every time I stepped from my tent. Both night and morning, I knelt next to my bed and prayed, begging Jehovah for Abraham's safe return. I knew I would hear from his servants if something had happened. No word came, so I tried to trust in Jehovah's care.

After almost three weeks, I returned to visit Isaac, begging him to travel to Paran to ensure Abraham had not been injured or fallen ill. Isaac comforted me as he bounced his youngest sister, Nogahh, on his lap as he spoke while Rebekah sat near me. "Father is well. I have received a witness he is neither sick nor injured. He is helping Ishmael overcome his great sorrow."

"Sorrow?" My eyebrows lifted in question.

"I saw him in a dream. He and Ishmael are building a place to lay Hagar's body." He rubbed Nogahh's back.

"At his age?" I cried.

"His servants are helping," Rebekah said. She turned to Isaac. "They are helping?"

"No. Father and Ishmael are building a small place to lay Hagar alone. They are doing it together, soothing their sorrows together."

I wiped a tear from my eye. "I knew Abraham would grieve at Hagar's death," I said, soothing the unborn child within me. "I heard him speak of her in his sleep. He regrets sending her and Ishmael into the desert."

Isaac moved Nogahh into Rebekah's lap and stood to pace the floor. Nogahh snuggled into Rebekah's arms.

"I know you think Father sent Hagar and Ishmael to the desert because Ishmael taunted Sarah."

"That is what everyone who was there says," I said.

Isaac shook his head and stopped pacing. "It was the right thing for us all. Father told me it needed to be done." He turned and paced to the edge of the tent, then returned to stand in front of me. "He missed the opportunity to teach Ishmael in his later youth and early manhood.

However, Ishmael needed to learn to depend on Jehovah. He could not learn that living here in our village, expecting to inherit all Father had. There was a reason for him to be sent away."

"It is good they work together to appease their grief together now," Rebekah said. "Ishmael needs to know his father loves him, that he loves his mother and him."

I nodded and stared at my hands, pleating my skirt. "At his age," I muttered.

"He will return to us with no injuries," Isaac added.

"You are certain?" I asked.

"I am certain. He will be exhausted, but he will come home soon."

Three days later, I sat in front of our tent spinning and watching when the guard at the top of the hill called a warning. Rebekah and Isaac joined me as I hurried to the edge of the village, where we could see who traveled the trail toward us.

Abraham rode tall in his saddle with no evidence of the arduous work he had completed with Ishmael, peering forward, as though seeking someone. When I stepped forward, his grin warmed my soul.

"He missed me," I breathed.

"You expected something else?" Rebekah asked.

"I feared he would stay with Hagar and Ishmael." I chewed on the inside of my mouth.

"But Hagar died," Rebekah cried. "Why would he want to stay away from you and your children? He looks forward to your unborn child."

I pushed a stray strand of hair behind my ear. "I do not know why. But I feared he would."

"He did not. Look. He rides toward you."

I lifted my face and stepped forward as Abraham pulled his horse to a stop and dismounted faster than I had seen him do in many years.

"Keturah!" he cried. "I have missed you." He wrapped me in his arms. I peeked over his shoulder at Rebekah, grinning.

"I told you he would," she mouthed.

I nodded and turned with him as he retrieved his walking stick and led me to our tent.

Twins

Before the time came for our next child to be born, Rebekah and Isaac brought us good news.

"After all these years," Isaac said, "Jehovah has filled Rebekah's womb with a child."

I glanced up at Rebekah. Her demur smile affirmed his words.

"Then you were with child when Abraham was gone?" I asked.

"Yes. Isaac believes I should rest each day to ensure the child stays within me."

"Abraham said the same thing to me in those first weeks when I carried Zimran. I had no problems with him, and Abraham learned I am strong enough to carry children without resting during the afternoon every day. Allow Isaac his concern. He can worry for you until he knows all will be well."

"I have so much to do to prepare," Rebekah said with a sigh. "It is difficult to spend time each day resting."

"I will help you as you helped me. I can weave and sew for your child as you helped me with clothing for mine. I have successfully learned to weave beautiful patterns effectively and accurately in these years since you taught me."

"You would do that? Your child will be born soon."

"I can help while I wait and as my child sleeps. I have done this before."

Rebekah nodded. "I wanted to do it all myself."

I remember wanting to do everything myself. I could not anymore than she could.

"But you helped me prepare for my first child," I argued. "I am happy to help you."

In the next two months before Shua's birth, I wove two blankets and made clothing for her baby. We sat together in the mornings working together on baby clothing.

All that ended one morning with Shua's birth.

After his birth, Refaela insisted I stay in bed longer than I wanted. I had given birth to seven other children already. Shua was my eighth child. I knew about babies and what they did to my body. However, Abraham sided with Refaela and encouraged me to stay in bed. I agreed to do so, though not cheerfully, because he asked, rather than demanding it from me.

While I sat in bed, watching Shua sleep, I stitched new clothes for Rebekah's baby. I had sewn new clothing for Shua in the early days I carried him. And I still had clothing from the other children. Rebekah did not have older children whose clothing she could use, so I helped her prepare for her child.

I watched Rebekah's body change during the early months she carried her child. It grew faster than I had, even with my eighth child. Every child stretched my stomach a little more. But Rebekah grew bigger than I ever did.

I had heard of women carrying more than one child at once. It did not happen often, but it happened. As big as her stomach grew, I wondered if Rebekah was one of those who did. It was not until she had been with child for six months that she admitted to me that Deborah had felt two babies within her.

"Two babes?" I asked. "Is that safe?"

She shrugged. "I know nothing about safe. I have not had one child before, certainly not two at once. I hope it is safe, for I carry two children, two sons."

Something about the way she said it made me stare into her face. "You heard something?"

If I had not been watching, I would not have seen her slight nod or the tinge of pink on her cheeks.

"I did. But it is sacred. I just know my sons will be born healthy."

I searched her face, then glanced at her enormous stomach. "Good. What can I do to help?"

"I will need more clothing and blankets for the boys. Are you able to help me?"

Shua whimpered in his little bed by my feet. I bent and patted his back. "I will be happy to help you. In the past years, I have learned to weave quickly and well."

"You will need to care for your children as well."

"Elia loves to help with Shua and Isbak. The older boys tag behind Zimran when he goes to the hills to herd the sheep and goats. I keep Midian home some days, but he cries to be with his brothers. Eila sometimes follows them into the hills, so she can be certain they are safe. I can weave and sew for you."

"Are you certain Eila only watches her brothers?"

"She does it so cheerfully, I have not asked her why." My gaze turned toward the hills. "Do you know something I should?"

"I have seen her walking with one of the boys, Danil."

"Danil?" My eyebrows knit together. "I do not remember a Danil. "Do you mean the herder boy who is Jokshan's friend?"

"Yes, I think that is the one. They walk home together from the hills most days. I would not know, but they pass my home each evening."

"And I thought she was there to watch her brothers." I pinched my lips together. What has my daughter been doing?

"Oh, I am certain she is watching the little boys as well," Rebekah hurried to say. "She is also watching Danil. Beware. You may have him asking to marry her."

"A herder?"

"What men are better? Our men are herders."

Shua cried. I lifted him from his bed and comforted him. As I patted his back and soothed him, I thought about my oldest daughter with a herder. *Why should I be upset? I would gladly have married a herder when I was young, before Sarah insisted Abraham marry me. I would have gladly married Ezra.*

"Danil?" I asked Deborah. "Is he not Ezra's son?"

"I believe so. You would have to ask Isaac or one of the men. Why?"

I sighed softly. "There was a time I thought I would become Ezra's wife. Before Abraham..."

"Before Sarah asked you to marry Abraham?"

I nodded and buried my face in Shua's little body.

"But you have been happy with Abraham. Have you not?"

I lifted my head. "I have. There are times I wonder what life with Ezra would have been like." I shook myself. "That is nothing I will ever know. It was not to be. My life is tied to Abraham now. If Danil asks for her, I will not argue."

Rebekah nodded.

"I will start another blanket for your children today."

Children Marry

As I wove another blanket for Rebekah's boys, I thought about Eila and Danil. It would be an interesting twist if she married Ezra's son. Did Ezra see it that way as well?

That afternoon, as I pushed my shuttle between the thread and left it there, Eila entered my weaving tent.

"May I speak with you, Mother?" she asked staring around the room.

"Certainly, you may. What would you like to speak about?"

"You have so many baskets of threads and yarns. What are you planning to weave?"

I cocked my head to the side. Surely she had not come to ask about my weaving projects. "I am weaving another blanket for Rebekah's boys."

"Boys? Is she certain there are two? How does she know they are boys?"

I lifted my hands to slow her questions. "Deborah felt two children within her. Rebekah says they are boys. I do not question her. What is it you wanted to speak to me about?"

"Danil asked me to marry him. Mother," her face twisted. "Will Father allow me to marry a herder's son?"

"Do you love him?" I asked, avoiding her concern.

She huffed out a big breath. "I do. Or I think I do."

I nodded. "Girls do not always know love. I had a similar problem as a girl. I thought I loved a boy my age."

"But you married Father. What happened to the boy?"

I shook my head. "Things happened. Your father was the man I needed to marry, although I thought I wanted to marry another."

"Who?"

I rolled my lips inward. "No. You need not know. It no longer matters. I have had many happy years with your father and I have eight beautiful children."

She looked at the floor, her desire to know battling with her need to obey me.

"Does this Danil love you?"

"He says he does. He says he does not want to wait like his father did. He wants to be certain he can marry me." She flopped to the floor and sat on her legs. "I do not know. This seems so rushed."

"How long have you been walking home from the hills with him?" I asked.

Her body jerked in surprise. "How did you know about that?"

I bent to pick little Shua from his bed to hide my giggles. "Rebekah told me about it yesterday. I saw the two of you yesterday. So, how long?"

She shrugged her shoulders, trying to look unconcerned. "A few weeks."

"And you did not trust your mother enough to tell me?" I feigned hurt. "I am happy for you."

"You are?" Her mouth dropped open for an instant before she closed it with a pop. "I thought you would be angry with me."

"Because a young man likes you enough to be certain you get home safely with your brothers?"

"Because I walked alone with him." Her chin dipped down. "But my brothers were always with me."

I nodded. "They will protect you."

"Danil is a good man. He is strong and brave. He never tries to touch me," Eila protested.

"I expected him to be a good man. His father was."

"You know Ezra?" Her eyes widened.

"I know most of the men in our village. We worship together. Ezra was our neighbor when I was young." I did not want to share the other intimate details of our relationship.

"Would you help me talk to Father about allowing us to marry?"

"That is for you and Danil. If your father asks me, I will add my approval."

Eila's lower lip extended for a moment before she grinned. "That is good enough for me." Her arms embraced her brother and me.

Unknown to either Eila or me, Abraham had watched Danil court her for many weeks. He had quietly waited for Danil to seek his permission to marry his daughter. The next Sabbath, I sat with him outside our tent the afternoon when Danil came over.

"I wondered when you would come to visit me," Abraham replied when the young man asked.

Danil spluttered. "We have been careful."

"I know. That is why I did not throw you out of the village."

I stared at Abraham. Would he really throw a young man out for his interest in his daughter?

"I love your Eila," Danil said. "She is young, and so am I. We will be a good couple, bringing many grandchildren into your life. We will be excellent parents."

"I have no doubt you will. Do you have a home for my daughter?"

"A ... home," he stammered, glancing at his feet. "Not yet, but I have skins I can use to make a tent."

"A big tent?" Abraham asked.

Danil's eyes returned to meet Abraham's. "I do not believe we will need a big tent at first. I will use my share of the lambs next season to trade for more skins. We will have a nice enough tent then."

"I cannot send Eila into your mother's tent. That would not be kind." Abraham lifted his hands to fend off Danil's arguments. "Your mother is a wonderful woman with a kind heart. But her tent is already full of your brothers and sisters. It would not be fair to her to bring another woman into her home. Nor would it be fair to Eila to have to go live with your brothers and sisters."

"But we can marry when I have a home for us?" Danil pressed.

Abraham glanced over to see me nod. "Yes. When you have a home."

Danil danced down the path toward his home, cheering.

"Do you think he should have shared the news with Eila?" I asked.

Abraham grinned. "I suspect she sat next to the tent door listening all this time. She would know my answer if she listened to his whooping."

Eila stepped through the tent door, her face bright red in embarrassment. "I did not think you would know I was there."

Abraham put an arm around her waist as she stood near him. "I would not expect you to be anywhere else, unless you did not want to marry him. Do you?"

Her eyes gleamed. "Yes, Father. I do want to marry Danil."

"Then you should be certain you have everything you need. I suspect you will not have much time to prepare. He will have a tent for you soon."

Eila had woven blankets and prepared other items for her home since she was old enough to weave, sew, and make baskets and pots. She had almost everything she would need, especially for a small tent. However, she used my loom to weave fabric to make a new dress for herself in the next weeks.

I used the time to sew baby clothes for Rebekah's babies. Eila, Rebekah, and I sat together and visited about marriage and babies. We teased Eila some about her marriage and Danil, but it was gentle, loving teasing.

Then, three weeks after asking Abraham to marry Eila, Danil returned with the news that her tent was ready. Abraham performed the marriage rite the following Sabbath.

With Eila gone, her brothers, Zimran, Jokshan, Medan, and Midian, brought home news they had found wives. They soon had tents made for their women and were married and out of our tent in less than three months. Our tent felt empty, with only Anath, Ishbak, Nogahh, and Shua to make noise.

In the middle of all the marriages, Rebekah gave birth to two boys, as she had told me she would. The first was red and hairy. They named him Esau. The second had held onto Esau's heel and came out almost as fast. This son they named Jakob. I suspected there would be a rivalry between the boys. There must have been rivalry, even within Rebekah's womb, for Jakob to grab Esau's heel.

Division

With fewer children in our home, I took little Shua to visit Rebekah as often as I could. The three boys played together happily for many years. Shua always seemed to be with them. I loved watching the three of them run and play, then follow the animals to the fields.

Since I had more time, Abraham encouraged me to remember and record the events of my life for our posterity.

"I am not virtuous," I said. "Shet ..."

"Was a wicked man. His actions did not destroy your virtue. He will pay for his choices. You will not."

I sucked in a deep breath. "Do you consider me virtuous?"

He took me into his arms. "I would not have married you if you were not virtuous. You are an exceptional woman."

In the time I spent writing the memories of my life, I included Shet's behavior toward me. My sons needed to know how that kind of behavior would hurt a man and the girl.

In the next years, Abraham shared with me his concern for his sons. "I have seen the arguments and the ugliness when sons strive to grow in a confined space. I saw it with the sons of Heth. I do not want to have the same thing happen to my children."

"What can we do?" I asked.

"I do not know." He ran his hands through his hair and huffed out his breath. "Something must be done for them. I cannot allow them to argue and hate one another."

I agreed with him. I had seen the same problems concerning him in other families. But these were my children. He had committed to Isaac as his birthright son. Isaac would receive the land and the rights of the family. What could my sons expect from their father? Would they consider family intrigue and dishonor to receive the blessings from their father? I hoped not.

We spent many hours in prayers together. I prayed when I was alone, carrying a prayer with me that Abraham could resolve the problem without sending my children and me away, as he had sent Hagar and Ishmael away. My heart hurt at the thought.

Then one day, when Shua was still young, perhaps ten, Abraham asked me to prepare a special feast and invite Isaac and all our married children to join us. By then, only Nogahh and Shua still lived in our tent with us.

We enjoyed visiting with all the children and grandchildren. All the while, the hurt in my heart continued. By now, I knew Abraham's plans, and although I agreed with them, they made me sad. I tried to smile and enjoy this day with all of our children. How would my children accept their father's counsel?

Then, Abraham gathered everyone close. "It is time to divide my goods," he said. "I have lived many years longer than I ever thought I would. I have more sons now than I expected. It took Sarah and me many decades to have Isaac born to us, so many years that I believed Ishmael would be my only son."

He gazed around at the gathering of children and grandchildren. "But then Jehovah fulfilled his promise and gave us Isaac." He reached out for Isaac's hand. Love filled his eyes for this promised son.

My stomach churned. Although there was no reason for it to churn, it did.

"I am blessed to be your son," Isaac said.

"And, after my Sarah died, I found Keturah," Abraham continued, seeking my hand. "She has been a blessing to me in my old age, blessing me with six sons and three daughters. Jehovah has richly blessed us."

I squeezed his hand. "Jehovah has blessed me with you."

After a moment of shared love, Abraham continued. "I love each of you, my children. However, I saw how envy can cause problems when Ishmael spoke of making Isaac his slave. I could not allow that and sent him and his mother into the east country. Although I would never expect Isaac to do the same, I will not be here much longer to protect you, my children from Keturah."

A shiver ran down my spine.

Zimran and his brothers inhaled and looked at each other. They had seen this coming.

"I would never consider enslaving my brothers," Isaac protested. "I love each of you."

I saw love in his eyes as they found each of my children who joined him in the circle of sons around their father, then at his sisters and the wives of his brothers, who sat just behind the men.

"No, you would not," Abraham said, shaking his shaggy head. "But each of these, my other sons, deserve a place where their families can spread out and grow." He turned to our oldest son and called his name. "Zimran?"

Zimran rose and stepped forward. Abraham turned to the stack of gifts he had prepared earlier and lifted gold and silver into his son's arms. "You are to take your family to the east where you can grow without concern for space and other people. Take Shua and your sisters and their families with you."

Shua gulped, but said nothing. Nogahh grabbed Eila's hand and held it tight.

Abraham continued as though unaware of the responses of his youngest children. "Protect them. Care for them. Find a wife for Shua and a husband for Nogahh who worship and love Jehovah."

"Not my babies!" I cried out. *I did not know he would send Shua and Nogahh away. I had hoped he would allow them to stay a few more years.*

Abraham took my hand and hushed me.

"Yes Father. I will care for Shua and my sisters and find them an honorable husband and wife." Zimram bowed his head to his father and sat back in his seat. His wife took his hand and squeezed it.

Zimran had been taught since he was tiny that Isaac would receive the birthright. He did not expect to receive it.

"Jokshan?" Abraham called.

Jokshan stood. "Yes. Father."

"Take this." Abraham bent again to reach Jokshan's gifts and handed them to him. He gave this son gifts much like those he gave to Zimran. "Go to the east country with your brother. Remember to care for your brothers and sisters. But do not live so close to them it causes you trouble. Remember, you will each need grass for your animals."

Tears slipped past my eyelids. I tried not to cause my children grief and wiped them away, hoping they would not see.

Jokshan bowed his head. "Thank you, Father. Your advice is excellent as always. I will remember."

Abraham called Medan next, giving him gifts and telling him to move to the east. He then spoke to Midian, Ishbak, and Shua, giving each of them gifts and advising them to go with their older brothers to the east where there would be room for their families to live safely in peace.

He called our daughters up last, Eila and Anath with their husbands, then Nogahh. He gave them gifts and called on them to listen to their brothers as they traveled east.

"Zimran will be the patriarch of your families," Abraham said. "Listen to him. He will do the right thing for you."

Abraham called each son forward, beginning with Shua, giving each of them a blessing of the good things of the world and calling on Jehovah to bless and care for them and their families through them.

To Zimran, he added the blessing of caring for his brothers and sisters and their families. "Remember Jehovah in all you do. Know that as you worship him, he will always bless you."

Last, he called Isaac to sit before him.

Isaac knelt before his father to receive his blessing.

"I give to you the lands surrounding Mamre and all the land of Canaan when Jehovah allows you to receive them. Remember the love we have for the kings and leaders of these surrounding countries. Zohar, his son, Ephron, and the sons of Heth. Although Jehovah has given us the land from Damascus to Egypt, we will not claim it until he gives us permission. Our neighbors have been good to us. We must continue to treat them well until Jehovah gives us permission to claim all the land."

Isaac nodded.

I bobbed my head, thinking of all the good that had come from our neighbors. Isaac needed to remember that.

By now, my tears dripped from my chin unheeded. My square of linen dripped. I had stopped trying to wipe them away. I was soon to lose all my children, and Isaac received all the land and all the blessings. I expected Isaac to receive these blessings, but my mother's heart hurt.

Abraham continued with his blessing. "I give you the birthright and all the blessings that come with it. You already care for our many animals and all our land. Continue to do this. All that belongs to this land is yours. Protect the men and women of our village. Move often enough to protect the land from overgrazing. Do not battle with other men unless Jehovah calls on you to protect yourself or those you love."

I sniffed. Zimran could do these things, but he was not the birthright son. Abraham was sending him away.

"Keep your family pure. Remind your sons to only marry women of the covenant who will love and honor Jehovah as you and Rebekah have. If it means you must send your sons back to Harran to find a woman to marry, do this, for to do any less would be to subject them to grief and pain."

I glanced at Shua. What of him? Would Zimran find him a woman who loved Jehovah to marry? Would he find a believer to marry Nogahh? What would Rebekah do for Esau and Jakob?

Abraham continued his instructions to Isaac. He then lay his hands on Isaac's head and blessed him with the blessings of Jehovah, including a large posterity who would love Jehovah and bless the earth.

Isaac would have a large posterity. Would he also require three wives to bring more children into his family? Would Jehovah give Rebekah more children? I sighed. *The birthright was Isaac's. It always had been.*

At the end of the blessings, Rebekah helped my maids and I serve the food we had prepared. I spent time with each of my sons and daughters and their families. The women chattered about their upcoming move. Some glanced away. I suspected they would miss their mothers. The men spoke in excitement of leaving the settled land of Canaan to find a home in the east. Although Abraham had not insisted they leave immediately, they were excited to find a new home and a new life. Zimran and Jokshan saw the need to expand.

All I could think was that my children would leave me.

"What will you do, Keturah?" Isaac asked sometime during the evening. "Will you be leaving with your children?"

"My life is here with Abraham."

Rebekah embraced me. "You will not be alone. We are here for you."

My face burned. "Thank you. I have depended on Zimran and the others for all these years. It will be difficult for them to be gone. But I understand Abraham's instructions. We have discussed this problem for many weeks before he called this meeting. I would not like our families to struggle with each other."

"Nor would I," Rebekah said.

"I would never make them my servants," Isaac said, spreading his hands out. "But their families are growing and need more space. I will miss them."

In the next weeks while they prepared, I went to the home of each of my children to help them pack their possessions into baskets and trunks. Isaac went through the herds of sheep, goats, cattle, and camels, dividing herds from the greater herd for each of his brothers and his sister's husbands. Each of the women had young women as maids. These young women joined my children.

Within two weeks, they were packed and marching out of our village. I never saw them again. Occasionally, over the next years, I allowed tears of sorrow to drip down my cheeks when no one was around to see.

Loss

As they became young men, Esau preferred to hunt wild animals while Jakob spent more time in the fields. I often wondered what Shua did. I would brush those thoughts aside and return to my chores. It did not help me to wonder.

One morning, in the year when Shua reached his sixteenth year, I woke with Abraham still laying beside me.

"Abraham," I cried. "Why are you not up and out with the animals?"

"I cannot rise," he mumbled, shaking his shaggy head. "I have no strength for it."

I hurried from our tent to Isaac's, calling for his help. "I cannot get your father to rise from his bed. I need your help."

"He is old," Isaac said as he hurried with me back to our tent. "I will see what we can do for him."

Isaac stepped to the bed and spoke with Abraham. "Are you well, Father?"

I moved to the other side of the bed and took his hand in mine.

"No, Isaac, my son. I will soon join your mother. You must send for Ishmael. I would give him a final blessing."

"And our sons?" I asked. "Should we send for them?"

Abraham coughed and fought for air. "No, Keturah. Our sons are far away. We cannot get a message to them in time. I gave them a final blessing before I sent them east. But Isaac, you need to know your brother. It is time."

Isaac gently lifted his father so he could sit in the bed. I spooned food into his mouth.

"I will send a messenger to Ishmael, then I will return," Isaac said.

Abraham waved his hand. "Send the message and care for the animals and your family. I will be with you for a few more days."

"And we want to spend much of those days with you," Rebekah said.

Abraham smiled and waved Rebekah closer to him. "Ah, Rebekah. You have been a blessing in our lives. How grateful I am you gave Amir and his camels water that day in Harran."

She bent and kissed him on the forehead. "I am grateful I did as well. It brought me to your home and to be your daughter."

"Go feed your family. You can return with them later." Abraham's voice had become weak and scratchy.

"We will return," she said, then turned to leave our tent.

"I have lived one hundred seventy-five years," Abraham said when we were alone once more. "I am the last of the generation of men after Noah. Men seldom live as long as me."

"I am grateful you have," I said, taking his tray away. I gave it to a maid and returned to sit beside him.

"You do not need to stay by my side," he said, sliding back down in the bed.

I pulled the covers to his chin. "I am here as I have always been, because I choose to be with you."

"Even though Sarah dragged your promise from you?"

"Even though. I am grateful she did. Our time together has been fulfilling. You gave me sons and daughters."

"You gave me sons and daughters. You cared for me at a time when I could not care for myself. I would not have lived this long if you had not become my wife. You have been good for me. I thank you."

"Would you give me one last blessing?" I asked.

"I will," Abraham said. "But not now. I do not have the strength. I must sleep first. Then I will bless you."

He woke later that afternoon with a clear mind. "You asked for a blessing?"

"I did. Can you give me one?"

"I can, if you come close where I can set my hands on your head."

I sat near the bed on a low stool where he could reach me with his hands and listened to his last sweet blessing. He had blessed me before, when I was about to give birth to another child or suffered from an ailment. This blessing was different. It was powerful. Even Abraham's voice strengthened as he spoke those words to me.

My children would also be a great nation, blessing the lives of those they met. My life was in the hands of Jehovah and I would be blessed.

"When you and my sons have buried me, call one of your sons to come for you. Go live with them. You deserve to live with your children," he counseled.

Tears streaked my face. Abraham knew my deepest desires. Jehovah knew me and what I needed. I would go, but not until after we had placed Abraham beside his beloved Sarah.

I wrote a letter to Zimran asking him to come to take me to live with him. When Rebekah came the next morning to sit with Abraham, I took my letter to a servant and asked him to find Zimran.

"I know generally where he is," the young man said. "I can find him."

"Do you know where we will be?"

"Isaac says we will move after the burial. I will return with Zimran before then."

I thanked him and returned to Abraham. I had so little time left with the man I loved, the father of my children.

When I returned to sit beside him, Abraham slept.

Rebekah and I spoke quietly together, neither of us wanting to leave him.

"He told me stories of our family, things I did not know about my grandmother."

"It must be wonderful to have family who can share stories with you."

"You do not remember your parents?"

"They left when I was young. They left me behind."

"Sad for you," Rebekah said.

"Not really. Mother did not care for me. Her husband used me. I was glad to see them leave."

Rebekah's arms surrounded me. "Your life has never been easy."

"Since I became part of Abraham's and Sarah's family, life has been easier. Agreeing to marry him was the best choice of my life. I will miss him," I murmured into her ear.

"We will all miss him, but not in the same way you will." Rebekah hugged me close before releasing me. "I do not know how I will live without Isaac. I hope he lives longer than me."

"For you, I hope so, too."

Ishmael arrived in the evening of the third day on a horse wet with lather from racing through the desert. Isaac brought him to be with Abraham soon after.

"It is good to meet you, Ishmael," I said. I motioned toward the sleeping room. "He waited for you to come." I pushed past the blanket separating our sleeping room from the rest of the tent.

I had washed him and combed his hair, making him presentable to see his first and lost son.

"I would not give my final blessing to you from my bed. Carry me into the sitting room?" Abraham asked.

His blessing on me was sacred and special, even given while he had lain in his bed.

Isaac bent to lift his father, but Ishmael gently pushed him aside. "Allow me?"

Isaac stepped aside while Ishmael lifted their father into his strong arms and carried him into the sitting area. Ishmael set his father on the long seat and tucked a blanket around him. Isaac and Ishmael squatted near their father, with Esau standing close.

I sniffed back my grief.

Jakob pushed through the tent door and stood next to Esau. I yearned to have Zimran and his brothers near me as well. It was not to be.

Abraham peered around the small circle of family. "I have waited a long time to have you all together again," he wheezed. Then he coughed.

I set my hand on his shoulder. Abraham shook himself, took a deep breath, and seemed to expand. The prophet in him filled him once more. He spoke with the powerful voice of the man I knew for so many years.

"I asked you to come so I could give you each my final blessing," he said.

"Not your last," Ishmael argued.

"Yes, son. My last. I will soon go the way of all the world. But before I do, I must give each of you a blessing. I have watched you both grow and become honorable men. I am proud of you."

Ishmael's eyes misted over. "You are proud of me?"

"I am, son. If you will come closer so I can reach you ..."

Ishmael moved a stool near his father and sat on it. Isaac and his sons sat on the floor to listen. Rebekah moved to kneel by Isaac's side. I stayed where I was, behind Abraham.

Abraham's blessing promised Ishmael great blessings as long as he remembered Jehovah and His grace in his life. The blessing continued longer than I expected. I sensed Jehovah's spirit strengthening Abraham.

When he pronounced his final amen, no one in the room had dry eyes.

Ishmael tenderly embraced his father until Abraham leaned back. "I have always loved you, son. I pray you and your descendants find peace with each other, as you now have peace together."

An intense glance passed between the brothers.

"We will do all we can to be friends," Ishmael said.

"We will," Isaac agreed.

They turned back to Abraham.

"While I can, it is your turn, Isaac," Abraham said.

Ishmael moved from the stool and sat close to his father while Isaac took his place.

Once more, Abraham lifted his quivering hands and set them on his son's head. Once again, Jehovah's spirit strengthen his voice as he pronounced a blessing on this beloved son. He promised posterity that would bless the lives of all who would believe in Jehovah, regardless of the time period in which they lived. He cautioned him to be at peace with all his brothers, offered him peace and blessings, and reminded him of Jehovah's love.

Once again, tears washed the faces of all present.

After embracing Isaac and before anyone said spoke, Abraham gestured for Esau to come sit on the stool.

I swallowed my concern that my sweet husband would not have the strength for this. Jehovah supported him. He would do well.

After blessing Esau, he gave Jakob a blessing.

He motioned to Rebekah.

"You are my beloved daughter, because Sarah could not have any. We had to send to Harran for you and have Isaac marry you." He tugged on her hand. "I would like to give you my final blessing."

She sat on the stool as he blessed her. He gave her a lovely blessing filled with love. It surprised me when near the end he added these words, "You will have the daughters you long for, whether they come from your body or come to you as you came to me. Jehovah knows the desires of your heart."

Tears flowed from Rebekah's eyes. "Thank you, dear Father Abraham," Rebekah stammered through her tears.

Tears flowed from my eyes as well. I prepared to take him back to his bed. Instead, he signaled for me to sit on the stool.

"You gave me a blessing already," I protested.

"Yes, but this will be my last husband's blessing. I must share with you."

I moved onto the stool and felt Jehovah's love through the words of my beloved husband. I would be blessed. My children would be part of blessing the world. Abraham loved me. I was satisfied.

At last, Abraham set his hands in his lap. "And now, my sons, I am finished. Help me to my bed. I will soon join my Sarah," he patted Isaac's hand, "and my Hagar," he patted Ishmael's.

Together, they lifted their father and carried him back to his bed.

Not long after they settled him on his bed, Abraham's eyes closed, never to be opened again in this life.

He slept for a while.

"Perhaps he will waken and share more with us," Ishmael said.

"Perhaps," Isaac said.

Women of the village brought food for us to eat as we sat in vigil. We waited and watched my beloved husband as he prepared to leave this earth. I held his hand in both of mine and whispered my love into his ear.

In a short time, Abraham trembled slightly and went still. He never moved again.

Isaac took his right hand, Ishmael took his left. I wanted to continue holding his hand, but gave it to his sons. I sucked in a deep breath and held it as we waited for his chest to lift again. It did not. I let the air silently out and watched as they held his hands a little longer, hoping his chest would rise once more with a shuddering breath.

It did not.

Finally, Isaac took the corner of Abraham's blanket and pulled it up. Ishmael took the other corner. They covered their father's face.

"He has gone home to Jehovah," Isaac said.

"To receive his reward," Ishmael said.

"To be with Sarah and Hagar," I added.

"Home," Rebekah breathed.

Abraham's Burial

I made a bed for myself in my weaving tent that night. I could not sleep in the bed where my beloved Abraham had put his arms around me and loved me. I would never sleep in that tent again.

Besides, Isaac and Ishmael were there inside, preparing his body for burial there.

I sat in front of my tent watching the moon move across the sky, remembering all the good things between us.

"Thank you, Sarah," I whispered into the night. I felt her there earlier, waiting with Hagar to escort our beloved husband home. "If you had not insisted, we would have missed the last years together. I would not have my sons and daughters. I thank you for sharing your good man with me."

Shouting rang out in the night from behind me. Ishmael and Isaac. It halted sharply. "No," Isaac shouted. "Hagar was his concubine. Sarah was his wife."

Their friendship faced problems already.

I shrugged. After we buried Abraham, I would leave them to resolve their problems.

I swallowed the lump that filled my throat. "Abraham, I miss you already."

I crawled between my blankets as the moon neared the western mountains. I would sleep later. I had spent much of the night writing these words, hoping my children would read them and know how much I loved their father.

My rest ended soon, as men loaded traveling tents on the camels, soon after an early breaking of our fast. Isaac and Ishmael came to me to ensure I was ready. I stood waiting for them in my traveling dress, a bag sat at my feet waiting to be loaded with the other baggage.

"We leave for Machpelah soon. Will you walk with us beside our father?" Isaac asked.

"I hoped you would ask me. I need one last walk with my beloved."

Ishmael put his big arms around me and held me close. "We will all miss him," he whispered in my ear.

I wrapped a scarf around my head to protect my hair and eyes. The walk would be dusty. Then I joined Abraham's sons as they lifted Abraham from his bed and moved him onto a sledge.

Jakob brought Abraham's white stallion to pull the sledge. I wondered if the riding horse would willingly pull a sledge. The horse nudged Abraham's body, then stepped in front, waiting to be hitched to it.

Jakob led the stallion. Isaac, Ishmael, and I walked beside the sledge toward the gathering place where we met Rebekah and Esau.

Our little family led the people of Mamre down the trail to Machpelah. Our thoughts were somber as we walked, interrupted often by Isaac and Ishmael remembering their father.

I stayed in my thoughts, only barely hearing the words the men spoke. They needed to remember their father. I would grieve in my own way.

We arrived at the cave of Machpelah near the end of the afternoon. The sun was already dropping behind the mountains.

"I will offer a sacrifice first," Isaac said. "We will then inter Father's body in the cave."

Ishmael nodded. "That is what Father did when we buried Mother. I expected that."

While the men of the village unpacked the tents and set them up, Isaac prepared for the sacrifice. I found a place away from the bustle and noise and sat beneath a tree, thinking of Abraham and how Jehovah must have met him the night before. It must have been an exciting time. Sarah and Hagar would have joined Jehovah in welcoming Abraham. I almost wished I could have been with him there. I missed him already.

When the altar was prepared, Jakob came to escort me to sit near the front. We sat on mats on the ground. Jakob held my hand as we observed the sacrifice. As Isaac lifted his hand to the ram, I saw Abraham beside him. He stayed until Isaac completed the sacrifice. I knew he had passed the responsibility of leadership of those who loved Jehovah to this son. My heart lifted. Abraham had earned his rest.

Jakob and Esau helped Isaac and Ishmael carry my beloved husband's body to the cave and set it gently beside Sarah's bones and stood back. They allowed me to lead the way. I stopped and touched his body.

"I love you, Abraham," I whispered. "Thank you both. You and Sarah gave my life a purpose."

Silent tears fell off my chin, unheeded. I stepped back as each of the others walked past to pay their respects. Rebekah and Isaac came at the end of the line.

"I will always love you, Father Abraham," she whispered. "You welcomed me into your family as a daughter. I will do all I can to honor your memory. Rest well."

I kissed Abraham one last time. "Sleep well, my love," I whispered. "I will join you soon."

Isaac prayed at the mouth of the cave, asking Jehovah to protect the cave and its occupants from predators and others who would desecrate it. The men filled the entrance with rocks. We would know where to find it when it was needed again. I hoped my sons would bring me here in the end.

If not, it did not matter. I would be with Abraham as Hagar was, even though their bodies were far apart.

We stayed near the cave for three days, sharing stories and love with Ishmael before he returned to his home. I returned to Mamre with Isaac and his family, knowing Zimran would soon be there to take me with him to my family.

I Leave

Zimran waited for my return in the nearly abandoned village of Mamre. When I dismounted from the horse brought for me to ride home, he took me in his arms and allowed me to sob.

I have gathered my possessions and as I write these last words, Zimran's men load them onto camels. I will leave my story with Sarah's stories, giving them to Rebekah. Perhaps one day, my children and Abraham's other descendants will read it and remember me. I do not want to be the lost wife of Abraham.

My life has been good. I pray my children remember their father as I do. I will miss him until I return to him.

I looked out the tent door. Zimran will be here for me soon. The sun rises into a red sky. What does it portend?

For the woman
who unexpectedly discovers
her virtue is accepted.

Acknowledgements

Another book you read!

I never planned to write this book. I don't think I even knew this woman existed, until reading the next verses in Genesis to get ready for the next book. I found five verses about this woman Abraham married. I hope you appreciate her story as much as I did.

I must always thank my patient sweetheart, Jack, for his support. Some days I sat at my desk, other days I sat beside him, often ignoring him, tapping my keyboard. Without his support, I would never get a book written.

My family always supports me. I am grateful for them. My mom and dad do all they can to help, and dad, who is now 96, is my final proofreader. Without my family's support, it would be much more difficult to write.

Another valuable support has been my ANWA (American Night Writers Association) support and sprinting groups. Writing as fast as I could for 30 minutes each sprint got much of this book written. Thanks especially to Carol Malone who encouraged me to write when I didn't feel like it.

As always, this would not be as good of a story without the efforts of my editor, Marsha Ward. With her careful editing, this book is more readable for you. Additionally, the fantastic skills of Dar Albert, who has created another beautiful cover for this book. I give both ladies my heartfelt thanks.

My AngelCAST team read the final version and found the last typos and mistakes that needed to be fixed. Thank you, team!

Last, but never least, a big thank you, goes to you, my reader, for choosing to read this book of fiction I wrote. I would love to hear how you liked it. Email me at Angelique@AngeliqueCongerAuthor.com.

Did You Enjoy This Book?

If you did, will you do something for me?

I'm an independent author, publishing my books without the backing of a major publisher. That means no six-figure advances and no advertising budget. This makes it difficult to promote my novels and put them in places new readers can find them. But you can help me.

Honest reviews and genuine "word-of-mouth" advertising makes all the difference. I'm not asking for one of those awful bookreports I used to try not to sleep through, that you did in school. What will help me is if you would leave an honest star rating and a couple of sentences on the bookseller's site where you purchased this book. Or a short review on your blog. Or tell your friends about it on your favorite social media site.

Let people know what you liked about this book and why they might like it, too. And, if there was something you didn't like, you can say that, as well. Constructive criticism helps me write a better book next time.

But, please. No spoilers!

Would You Like a Free Book?

If you have not yet agreed to receive my weekly newsletter, Angelique's Historical Fiction Reader, maybe now would be a great time to join. If you want to read the short story about Shamgar, the healer who helped Ziva and Crites, click here[1] to receive Damaged Healer.

If you would like a short story about Eve assisting Adam, click here[2] to receive Avenging Angel.

If you currently receive my weekly newsletter and did not receive one of these free books, let me know. I'll be happy to forward you a link for either book.

Angelique@AngeliqueCongerAuthor.com

Happy Reading,

Angelique

1. https://dl.bookfunnel.com/ldg1thkpcj

2. https://dl.bookfunnel.com/to6h2blg9y

Books by Angelique Conger

Ancient Matriarchs

Eve, First Matriarch

Into the Storms: Ganet, Wife of Seth

Finding Peace: Rebecca, Wife of Enos

Moving into Light: Zehira, Wife of Enoch

Out of Darkness: Imma, Wife of Noah

We Stood Beside Them: Other Wives of the Patriarchs

Lost Children of the Prophet

Lost Children of the Prophet

Captured Freedom

Abandoned Hope

Brotherly Havoc

Betrayed Trust

Convicted Deliverance

Trouble Escaped

Contrary Devotion

Imapssioned Grief

Love Defied

Hidden Purpose

Concealed Innocence

Struggle for Limhah

Combating Cults

Fighting Foreign Armies

Defending Faith

Into Egypt

About the Author

Many would consider Angelique Conger's books Christian focused, and they are because they focus on early events in the Bible. She writes of a people's beliefs in Jehovah. However, though she's read in much of the Bible and searched for more about these stories, not finding much to help, her imagination fills in the missing information, which is most of it.

Angelique Conger discovered the wonders of writing books later in her life. Books, however, have always been important to her. As a little girl in a small town, she received a library card of her own at the tender age of five, unusual in those days.

Angelique reads a book, or three at once, much of the time. She reads most genres of books and, until a few years ago, only toyed with writing them. Since beginning, she has spent many hours each day learning the craft of writing and editing.

Angelique lives in Southern Nevada with her husband and two cats, who share love by sharing her pillow and sleeping at her feet. She enjoys visits from her grandchildren and their parents.

Don't miss out!

Visit the website below and you can sign up to receive emails whenever Angelique Conger publishes a new book. There's no charge and no obligation.

https://books2read.com/r/B-A-NFPH-RDOED

BOOKS 2 READ

Connecting independent readers to independent writers.

www.ingramcontent.com/pod-product-compliance
Lightning Source LLC
LaVergne TN
LVHW010101110826
845155LV00028B/433